William John Fitzpatrick

Memoirs of Richard Whately

William John Fitzpatrick

Memoirs of Richard Whately

ISBN/EAN: 9783744660358

Printed in Europe, USA, Canada, Australia, Japan

Cover: Foto ©Raphael Reischuk / pixelio.de

More available books at **www.hansebooks.com**

MEMOIRS

OF

RICHARD WHATELY,

Archbishop of Dublin.

WITH A GLANCE AT HIS COTEMPORARIES & TIMES.

BY

WILLIAM JOHN FITZPATRICK, J.P.,

AUTHOR OF

"LADY MORGAN, HER CAREER, LITERARY AND PERSONAL;" "THE LIFE,
TIMES, AND COTEMPORARIES OF LORD CLONCURRY," ETC.

IN TWO VOLUMES.
VOL. II.

LONDON:
RICHARD BENTLEY, NEW BURLINGTON STREET,
PUBLISHER IN ORDINARY TO HER MAJESTY.
1864.

The Author reserves the right of translation.

ANECDOTAL MEMOIRS

OF

ARCHBISHOP WHATELY.

———◦◦◦———

CHAPTER I.

WITH the Calvinistic portion of his flock Dr. Whately early fell into deep disfavour by a general " Pooh! pooh!" of their principles; and still deeper, at a later period, by his " Thoughts on the Proposed Evan- " gelical Alliance." With this self-consti- tuted body, having mainly for its object " the Propagation of the Gospel," Dr. Whately, for due reasons assigned, not only refused to co-operate, but admonished his clergy neither to join nor countenance it.

" I am sure," he writes, " I did not fail " to give credit for good intentions to the

" individuals generally who have set on foot
" and joined in such associations as the
" Evangelical Alliance. And I might have
" added, that from the very first, long before
" the alarm now felt by them and by many
" other Protestants had arisen, I had pointed
" out the existing tendency towards those
" dangerous principles, which have since
" been openly avowed; and I have always
" continued, in defiance of all opposition
" and obloquy, actively, openly, and steadily
" to denounce those principles."

And in a letter from the Archbishop's
private secretary, Dr. West, published at
the same time by authority of his Grace,
the Evangelical Alliance is stigmatized as
"plainly schismatical!"*

Dr. Whately, in this pamphlet, neatly ela-
borated Shakspeare's apophthegm, that " the
" wish is father to the thought."

" Some doctrine, suppose, is promulgated,
" or measure proposed, or mode of pro-
" cedure commenced, which some members
" of a party do not, in their unbiassed judg-

---

* "Thoughts," pp. 5—15.

" ment, approve. But any one of them is
" disposed, first to *wish*, then to *hope*, and
" lastly to *believe*, that those are in the
" right whom he would be sorry to think
" wrong. And in any case, where his judg-
" ment may still be unchanged, he may feel
" that it is but a *small* concession he is
" called on to make, and that there are
" *great* benefits to set against it; and that,
" after all, he is perhaps called on merely to
" *acquiesce silently* in what he does not quite
" approve; and he is loath to incur censure,
" as lukewarm in the good cause, as pre-
" sumptuous, as unfriendly towards those who
" are acting with him. To be 'a breaker-
" 'up of the club' (ἑταιρίας διαλυτης) was a
" reproach, the dread of which, we learn
" from the great historian of Greece, carried
" much weight with it in the transactions of
" the party warfare he is describing.

" And when men have once been led to
" make one concession, they are the more
" loath to shrink from a second, and a third
" costs still less."—(Pp. 10, 11.)

The cupidity and nepotism of some influential members of the Evangelical Alliance, including a bishop still living, greatly disgusted Dr. Whately, who was an antidote to both.

The complete absence of gloom in the Archbishop, even on the Sabbath-day, also gave offence to the Calvinistic portion of his flock, and neither could they forgive his generous and genial inculcations of a moderate indulgence in pleasurable occupation on Sundays; with children he went farther, and urged that sports should engross a large share of their attention on the Lord's-day.

The manners of many Protestants, he considered, had a " manifest tendency to " associate with that festival ideas of gloom " and restraint, and also to generate the too " common notion, that God requires of us " *one only* day in seven, and that scrupulous " privation on that day will afford licence for " the rest of the week. We are speaking, " be it observed," he added, " of the " Christian festival of the Lord's-day; those " who think themselves bound by the pre- " cepts of the Old Testament relative to the

" Sabbath, should remember that Saturday is " the day to which those precepts apply."*

Deeper and deeper Whately sank in some evangelical estimations, especially when it became known that he had surrounded his palace by a moral fosse, which no intrigue could scale. All attempts to gain preferment by the irregular influences too often brought to bear upon bishops failed signally. To intermeddlers, Dr. Whately was inaccessible. Though sometimes moved by caprice, he never permitted external influences to guide him in his appointments.

A Roman Catholic ex-Commissioner of National Education, to whom we are indebted for not a few anecdotes, tells us that he was surprised to find himself stopped in the street by a Protestant clergyman, personally unknown to him, who, with considerable warmth, begged his acceptance of great gratitude for some preferment which Dr. Whately had given him. The eyes of our informant opened wide and still wider during the delivery of these cordial declara-

* " Lectures and Reviews," p. 325.

tions of thanks, which, he more than once exclaimed were utterly undeserved by him.

" You are mistaken, my dear sir," replied the clergyman. " I am indebted entirely to " you. Do you remember five years ago " incidentally mentioning with praise the " character which I bore in —— ? My " Archbishop quietly made a note of your " unpremeditated report, which he well knew " was disinterested, and to that circumstance " I may thank my appointment."

Dr. Whately continued to write on intricate questions of theological speculation, going too far, according to some ecclesiastical critics, and not going far enough in the estimation of others.

Dr. Whately did not enter the lists of controversy with his opponents; but, by way of weakening some of the imputations with which they pelted him, he published " The " Kingdom of Christ delineated in Two " Essays on our Lord's own account of his " Person, and of the Nature of his Kingdom, " and on the Constitution, Powers, and " Ministry of a Christian Church, as ap- " pointed by Himself." Though incorrect

in some points, the first part of this book
contains an able argument for the Saviour's
divinity.

" These are the positions," writes the
Archbishop, " which I have put forth from
" time to time, for many years past, in vari-
" ous forms of expression, and supported by
" a variety of arguments, in several different
" works, some of which have appeared in
" more than one edition. And though oppo-
" site views are maintained by many writers
" of the present day, several of them pro-
" fessed members of the Church of England,
" I have never seen even an attempted refu-
" tation of any of those arguments."

Bishop Copleston wrote to Dr. Whately
to say that he thought this book his best.
It has since run through five editions. Dr.
Whately, in colloquial commentary on his
theological censors, has been heard to say,
that if they read the second of his Bampton
Lectures, on the " Declaration of God in
" His Son," they would find evidence of the
orthodoxy of his views with respect to the
Person of Christ, on which he has oftentimes
been charged with holding erroneous senti-

ments.   In the Deity of Christ Whately was
a believer on logical principles.

"Jesus was tried, in the first place, before
" the Jewish Sanhedrim," he writes, " and
" was found guilty of blasphemy, because He
" confessed himself ' the Son of the living
" ' God.'   By this title the Jews understood
" Him to claim a divine character, and upon
" his own confession they adjudged Him
" worthy of death.   Unless, therefore, we
" conceive Him capable of knowingly pro-
" moting idolatry,—unless we can consider
" Jesus himself as either an insane fanatic or
" a deliberate impostor claiming divine honour
" not belonging to Him,—unless we come to
" a conclusion involving a difficulty so re-
" volting to all notions of Divine purity, and
" indeed of common morality, that all diffi-
" culties on the opposite side are as nothing,
" we must assign to Him, ' the Author and
" ' Finisher of our Faith,' the only-begotten
" Son of God, who is one with the Father,—
" that divine character which He and his
" apostles so distinctly claimed for Him ; and
" acknowledge that ' God ' truly ' was in
" ' Christ reconciling the world unto Himself.'

" In short, if we would believe in Him at all,
" we must believe in Him as perfect God no
" less than perfect man."

For severity of argument, Dr. Whately has
rarely been surpassed, and some dignitaries
of his own Church, when they found it difficult to refute his logical deductions,—formed
on the Anglican right of private judgment,—
retorted on him with much clamour, and
many bad names. " He is imbued with the
Sabellian heresy ! " shrieked one. " And
with the Pelagian ! " chimed in another ;
" and if the Council of Ephesus were now
" sitting, he would be certainly pilloried."
" The man is a Socinian—down with him—
" away with him ! " was ejaculated around.

" He disdains the trodden footpath of
" common everyday controversy," exclaimed
a lusty voice from the University ;* " he does
" not bring forward the texts adduced by
" Calvinists or predestinarians, and demolish
" them one by one after the fashion of the
" most approved but commonplace contro-

* " A Reply to Archbishop Whately's Essay on
' Election,' or Predestination to Eternal Life."

" versialists.   No—he boldly strikes out, and
" follows up a new and hitherto untrodden
" pathway for himself.   And while particu-
" larizing very little, but generalizing a good
" deal, he confidently asserts that the Cal-
" vinists have, all their life up, been occu-
" pying a faulty stand-point, in receiving
" into their creed a doctrine which is, 'if
" 'rightly viewed, of a purely speculative
" 'character not *belonging* to us practically,
" 'and which *ought* not at least in any way to
" 'influence our conduct;' and while he as-
" serts that 'he waives the question as to the
" 'truth or falsity of the Calvinistic doctrine'
" —the whole pith and marrow, and aim,
" and drift, and life-blood of the entire Essay
" is, to show up its faultiness and falsity, and
" to strip it of its slightest pretension to be,
" in any way, a Divine revelation.

  " This mode of attack, for attack it is, from
" a masked battery, is such as to present to
" the eye of the non-superficial reader a
" strong and ceaseless undercurrent of de-
" cided hostility against the doctrine in all
" its bearings—is the more dangerous, be-
" cause of its novelty—and to many might

" seem so strong in its strangeness and
" originality, and so profound in its train of
" thought, and so lucid in its arrangement,
" as to be totally unanswerable, and to settle
" the disputed point at once and for ever."

But the Calvinistic critic seems to think
that he can crush the Archbishop, and accordingly arranges his sling for the struggle.

All this clamour Whately surveyed with the
most provoking impassiveness. Unheeding
the storm, and wrapping his cloak still tighter
about him, he steadily continued the course
which he had proposed to himself to follow.

Dr. Whately's speeches in the House of
Lords were few and forcible, the cavils of
a " Random Recollector " notwithstanding.
He was always clear, generally pithy, and
eschewed all such phrases as " one word
" more and I have done."* His speech on
the Jews' Relief Bill was one of his best. He
began by declaring that he would not occupy
their Lordships' time by protestations of the

* " How we dread to hear this expression from the
" lips of a speaker at public meetings ! " said a jaded
newspaper reporter ; " it's always a sure sign that he's
" bracing up for a fresh start."

sincerity of his attachment to Christianity. " Such protestations receive, in general, but " little credit; and deserve little, unless they " are borne out by the general conduct of " those who make them; and, if they are, I " consider them superfluous." The Archbishop, in this speech, confined himself to the consideration of objections, because, if these were removed, the Bill ought to pass. In advocating the removal of Jewish disabilities, he remarked that he differed much more from persecuting Christians than he did from Jews, because the first acted in diametrical opposition to their creed, whereas the latter firmly supported theirs. The measure of relief urged in this speech came promptly to pass—an observation which may be said equally to apply to his " Thoughts on " Secondary Punishments " and " Remarks " on Transportation," in two letters addressed to Earl Grey.

We believe that it was in the latter pamphlet that Dr. Whately, with his wonted vehemence, pronounced the whole of Australia to be the descendants of convicts; and we have heard it stated that, in order to mark

their pique of such a stigma, not one of Dr. Whately's educational works were ever suffered to enter its shores ; but this report is at variance with some views recently expressed by Mr. Robert Torrens, Registrar-General of South Australia, who says that " the inhabit-
" ants of these colonies entertained sentiments
" of the highest veneration and gratitude
" towards the Archbishop for his services
" rendered to them in freeing them from the
" contamination of the criminal population of
" England, which was being poured on their
" shores. Almost the last act of the Arch-
" bishop was one in furtherance of this object.
" When a report on the subject of transpor-
" tation was laid before the Statistical Society,
" the Archbishop, although extremely feeble
" in health, visited them to arouse them to
" the importance of the question."

The ticket-of-leave system found little favour in the Archbishop's sight ; and he lost no opportunity to make a cut at it, and if he could contrive to make the sarcasm cut two ways, the joke was all the pleasanter. The Rev. Mr. M'Naught and others, having forsaken the Anglican Church, joined the

Sectaries, and finally came back to the Anglican Church again, Dr. Whately quietly remarked, "I hope they are not going to "send us ticket-of-leave clergymen."

The Archbishop would seem to have been averse to all capital punishments, which he regarded as anything but a capital cure for crime. "Every instance," he said, "of a "man's suffering the penalty of the law, is an "instance of the failure of that penalty in "effecting its purpose, which is, to deter."

In the social circle he continued to be the idol of the few rather than of the many. He "delighted in the oddities of thought, in queer "quaint distinctions," observed a gentleman who knew him well; "and if an object had by "any possibility some strange distorted side "or corner, or even point, which was under- "most, he would gladly stoop down his mind "to get that precise view of it; nay, would "draw it in that odd light for the amusement "of the company."

M. Guizot, the eminent French statesman, has recorded a curious impression of his introduction to Dr. Whately :—"Amongst "the English prelates with whom I became

" acquainted, the Archbishop of Dublin, Dr.
" Whately, a correspondent of our Institute,
" both interested and surprised me. His
" mind appeared to me original and well
" cultivated; startling and ingenious rather
" than profound in philosophic and social
" science; a most excellent man, thoroughly
" disinterested, tolerant, and liberal; and, in
" the midst of his unwearying activity and
" exhaustless flow of conversation, strangely
" absent, familiar, confused, eccentric, ami-
" able, and engaging, no matter what un-
" politeness he might commit or what pro-
" priety he might forget. He was to speak
" on the 13th of April, 1840, in the House of
" Lords, in reply to the Archbishop of Can-
" terbury and Bishop of Exeter, on the
" question of the Clergy Reserves in Canada.
" 'I am not sure,' said Lord Holland to me,
" 'that in his indiscreet sincerity he may not
" 'say he sees no good reason why there
" 'should be a bench of bishops in the House
" 'of Peers.' He did not speak, for the
" debate was adjourned; but on that occasion,
" as on all others, he would certainly not
" have sacrificed to the interests of his order

" the smallest particle of what he regarded as
" true, or for the public good."*

That "indiscreet sincerity" is often an attribute of true genius is indisputable.   And,
on the other hand, it has been remarked by
Lord Brougham of the Earl of Liverpool, that
his mediocrity of talents was joined to " its
" almost constant companion, an extreme
" measure of discretion in the use of them."†

The Archbishop was an odd man in many
ways.   He did not like people to ask him to
dinner for the purpose of making a lion of
him during feeding-time.   Those who ven-
tured to do so, often got an ominous dash of
his great mane in their face.   If he thought
that people tried to make him a buffoon, no
bust of Socrates could appear more grave.
Clumsily try to draw him out, and he at once
shut up.   And hereby hangs a tale.

The King of the Belgians having heard an
animated description of Dr. Whately's conversational powers, which he was anxious to

---

* "Embassy to England in 1840," by M. Guizot.
  † "Statesmen of the Time of George III." second
Series, vol. i. p. 171.

test, favoured him, when passing through
Belgium, with an invitation to dinner at
Lacken. The Archbishop, to the surprise
of every one, and to the special disappointment of the King, maintained, throughout the evening, a complete impassiveness.
Pegs were dropped, but the Prelate folded himself in reserve and refused to hang his usually
ready wit upon them. It was time to say
something, and Dr. Whately, when about to
take leave, said, "Your Majesty has done infinite
" mischief to all the kingdoms of the earth !"
Leopold smiled a ghastly smile, while some
officious listeners, with, as they themselves
thought, much tact, made an attempt to turn
the conversation. " My reason," said the
Archbishop, " for saying that your Majesty
" has done infinite mischief to all the king-
" doms of the earth is, because you have
" taught your people the blessings of an
" elective monarchy."

Sheridan, when asked what sort of wine he
preferred, replied, " Other people's." It was
not a joke which could come with truth from
Whately, who seldom if ever dined abroad, and
was never so happy as when presiding at the

head of his hospitable table, round and round which every sort of good wine sped and flowed.

Indeed, whatever "difficulties" Dr. Whately found in " the writings of St. Paul," he found no difficulty in interpreting, in the most practical manner, that passage wherein Paul declares that bishops should be hospitable. " He dispensed not only to his clergy," writes one of them, " but to a large circle of friends, " a constant and dignified hospitality."

No strait-laced whine ever penetrated these festive meetings. The fullest unreserve and the heartiest enjoyment reigned around. Fun, almost juvenile in its exuberance, was as often the order of the evening as logical puzzles or metaphysical speculations; and trying who should make the worst pun quite as frequently occurred as higher tests and tournaments of wit. At a farewell dinner to Dr. ——, Bishop Elect of Cork, a bottle of rich old Waterloo port, instead of making a rapid circuit, rested before him. " Come, ——," cried the Archbishop from the head of the table, " though you *are* John Cork, you mustn't " *stop* the bottle here."

The reply attributed to the Bishop was quite in the Whateleian vein. " I see your " Grace is disposed to *draw me out*. But, " though *charged* with *cork*, I'm not going to " be *screwed*."

" We are all most anxious to see you " *elevated*," exclaimed the host. " I leave " to your Grace, as a disciple of Peel, the " privilege of *opening* the *ports*," was the reply.

A higher order of wit more usually prevailed, and it is no wonder that the general impression of these dinners at the Palace should be so pleasant.

" Any one who has ever had the happiness " of passing an evening with the Archbishop, " or in his company, cannot soon forget the " pleasures of the privilege. His mirth was " enlivening, his raillery searching, his wit " sometimes sparkling, and his conversational " powers marvellous. He was something of " a monopolist where talk was concerned. " We once heard him contending with a " loquacious prelate for exclusive possession " of the audience; but it was the mountain " torrent meeting the tiny rill. He was

" occasionally comparatively silent where he
" wished to collect opinions on some subject
" on which he was writing. Whatever he
" could thus glean he would embody into
" his work, most frequently in the form of
" objections. Silence on his part was indeed
" the exception, and not the rule."

" Two of a trade never agree;" and we
believe it was of Dr. Whately that Sydney
Smith, who was himself a marvellous talker,
once said, in reply to a remark, that the former
appeared to great advantage in conversation,
" Yes, there were some splendid flashes of
" silence."

" A favourite play with Dr. Whately,"
writes a correspondent, " was pencilling a
" little tale on paper, and then making his
" right-hand neighbour read and repeat it,
" in a whisper, to the next man ; and so on
" until everybody round the table had done
" the same. But the last man was always
" required to write what he had heard ; and
" the matter was then compared with the
" original retained by his Grace. In many
" instances the matter was hardly recogniz-

" able, and Dr. Whately would draw an
" obvious moral; but the cream of the fun
" lay in his efforts to discover where the
" alterations took place. His analytical
" powers of detection proved, as usual,
" accurate, and the interpolators were play-
" fully pilloried."

At an auction of the Archbishop's effects,
in December, 1863, it awakened some emotions to see his Grace's fine stock of wines
sold by Cant, and distributed in unpenurious
samples among the unwashed, who, impelled
by curiosity, had come to the sale, but left
nothing except innumerable expectorations
on the Palace carpets. Coarse voices and
coarser jokes, stimulated by liquor, soon
became unpleasantly loud, and awakened, as
we have said, strange emotions, when con-
trasted with the feast of reason and the flow
of soul which had so often filled the same
apartment. The scene to which we allude
took place in the dining parlour, where the
Archbishop's wine-glasses, drinking chalices,
silver dish-covers, plates, decanters, coasters,
liquor-stands, and other relics of bygone con-

viviality were huddled together in promiscu-
ous confusion.*

Archbishop Whately was more closely
identified with, and more largely influenced
the political history of Ireland, during an
eventful period in her annals, than might,
perhaps, be cursorily supposed. He was a
sort of *ex-officio* Viceroy, who from the
year 1831 always acted as one of the
Lords Justices during the absence of the
Lord Lieutenant. His colleagues in the
government were frequently Plunket, Bushe,
Lord Morpeth, and Drummond. There are
some little incidents interwoven with the
more important proceedings of Dr. Whately,
in his capacity of Lord Justice, which it may
be amusing to notice, in passing. There is
extant a warrant, dated in 1837, and signed
by Archbishop Whately and Lord Plunket,
ordering the detention at the Dublin Post
Office of the letters of O'Connell and other
persons who, during that stormy period, were

---

* Leaving the dining-room, we saw the Archbishop's
fine travelling carriage—built by Hutton—sold for £11,
and his dog for as many pence !

suspected of a seditious correspondence. Many letters were opened and copied, and with such dexterity was the process performed, that no suspicion of this surreptitious exploration seems to have been for many years after awakened. To the application of steam the seals or wafers unresistingly succumbed; impressions had been previously taken of the seals; and there were men on the spot cunning in the art of resealing. If, in some conceptions, Dr. Whately erred in signing a warrant for effecting the examination of private correspondence, it must be admitted that he erred in good company; as there are also in existence similar warrants issued by Lords Anglesey, Wellesley, Hatherton, Mulgrave, Ebrington, De Grey, and others. So recently as the year 1858, when the Phœnix Conspiracy attracted the vigilance of Lord Eglinton's Government, the letters which passed between the sympathizers with that movement and the conductors of a popular newspaper were opened, read, " sealed and delivered."

The Archbishop made a joke on one of the many occasions that he presided as Lord Justice, which we may venture to give. An

old custom is still in vogue of compelling the
Lord Justice, on every consecutive occasion
that he enters on the duties of that office, to
go through a long-winded oath and formula.
" This is rank folly," exclaimed Dr. Whately,
at last losing all patience; "it would be just
" as reasonable to compel a man to go
" through the marriage ceremony every time
" he enters his wife's chamber."

The Archbishop's name does not appear at
the foot of the memorable De Grey Proclamation,* which brought the Repeal agitation

---

* As illustrative of a forthcoming remark, an extract
from *Raikes' Journal* may be given :—" When we were
" assembled in the drawing-room, before dinner, the Duke
" of Wellington entered, with the proclamation issued at
" Dublin Castle, to repress the Repeal meeting at Clontarf,
" on the 8th instant, which he had just received from town
" by express. He seemed very much elated, and, putting
" on his spectacles, read the whole proclamation out
" loud from beginning to end. 'They give us now a
" ' fair pretence to put them down, as their late placard
" ' invites the mob to assemble in military order, and
" ' their horsemen to form in troops. This order, pro-
" ' bably, was not written by O'Connell himself, but by
" ' some eager zealot of his party, who has thus brought
" ' the affair to a crisis. Our proclamation is well
" ' drawn up, and avails itself of the unguarded opening
" ' which O'Connell has given us to set him at defiance.' "

to a crisis, in 1843; although the names of
several other Privy Councillors are appended
to it. We have reason to know, however,
that he was by no means an unobservant
or unconcerned spectator of the political
events of that pregnant period; and, although
opposed to the prosecution of O'Connell, he
was equally opposed to a surrender of the
great measure for which O'Connell struggled.

" To expect," he said, " to tranquillize and
" benefit a country by gratifying its agitators,
" would be like the practice of the supersti-
" tious of old, with their sympathetic powders
" and ointments; who, instead of applying
" medicaments to the wound, contented
" themselves with *salving the sword* which
" had inflicted it."

But he would have his joke at the expense
of the prosecutors, and publicly too. It was,
and we believe still is, customary at the
Model School, in Marlborough Street, to
marshal the boys every morning, in a form
by no means dissimilar to the military rank
and file. While going through their evolu-
tions one day at this time, the Archbishop
was observed in the distance affecting the

most violent manifestations of excitement
and alarm. The Inspector, deserting his
post, ran to Dr. Whately for an explanation.
" Ho, ho," he said, " military order and
" array. If Mr. Attorney-General T. B. C.
" Smith, or his myrmidons, catch you, you
" will just catch it, I promise you."

If averse to intimidation on the popular
side, he pitted himself with still greater firmness against the Orange ovations, in which
that once intolerant ascendancy were prone
to indulge. When Dr. Whately first came
to Ireland, he found traces of an old and
silly fashion, of dressing and daubing the
statue of William III. in College Green—a
ceremony often attended with midnight dis-
order and outrage. By the presence of his
powerful muscle and sinew, he contributed
largely to strangle the serpent of discord,
and to obliterate the slimy cycles of its progress. In an unpublished letter to Bishop
Copleston, written shortly after his assumption of the reins of Dublin, Dr. Whately
denounces these odious practices. And, in
reference to the fashion of painting the statue
and its pedestal in the vulgar brilliancy of

orange and blue, he adds, "even the Pagans "would never paint a trophy."

The letter in which this passage occurs is one of many which Bishop Copleston's widow returned to Dr. Whately some years ago; and at a future day they may see the light.

The Rev. Charles Dickinson, having acted very efficiently as private Secretary to Dr. Whately, and evinced, in his intercourse with him, the powers of no ordinary mind, combined with the most self-forgetting modesty, was promoted—partly in compliment to the high estimate formed of him by his Grace, and partly in recognition of the broad liberality of his views—to the see of Meath, then vacant by the death of Bishop Alexander. The Consecration Sermon was preached on the 27th December, 1840, by Dr. Whately. Dr. Dickinson proceeded to his diocese; but while engaged in writing his primary charge, he was cut off by mortal illness. In the events which followed we have abundant evidence of that generous kindliness of disposition which the Archbishop strove, too often successfully, to conceal. He treated the bishop's widow muni-

ficently; provided for his sons in offices
connected with the Church; and in the following letter, for which we are indebted to
the recording hand of Dean West, testified
the strong emotions of grief and sympathy
which filled him. It is addressed to the
present rector of Narraghmore :—

"*July* 15*th*, 1842.

" My dear Charles,—

" I address you as the eldest son of
" my beloved friend, and as one (though not
" the only one) old enough to apply to a
" profitable use the sharp lesson you have
" received.

" It is not, certainly, the lesson we, in our
" short-sighted judgment, should have chosen
" for you, or for myself; but it is for us to
" *learn the lesson* that is set us by our
" heavenly Teacher, who has assured us that
" ' all things work together for good to them
" ' that love Him.' If we acknowledge this
" only when we *see how* things work together
" for good; if we can say, ' Thy will be
" ' done,' only when God's will happens to
" concur with ours, our faith in Him is
" nothing; we have our religion for nothing;

" for the humblest of our fellow-creatures
" may expect us to approve of, and acquiesce
" in, His decisions, when they just fall in with
" our own.

" But you have learnt, if it be not very
" much your own fault, a better lesson : for,
" ' Thy kingdom come ; Thy will be done,'
" was a text on which your father's whole
" life was the best of sermons.

" I am not going, therefore, to tease you
" with those topics of consolation which you
" must have learned from him—I have need
" of all my efforts to apply them for
" myself. What he was to me, God and I
" only know; and I feel that to indulge any
"selfish grief for a private friend, when the
" Church has sustained such a loss, would
" be very unlike his public-spirited character.

" But I wish to put before you some re-
" marks on the points in his character which
" may be made the most profitable to all of
" you as an example. It is a most pre-
" cious legacy, if you use it aright ; for I am
" sure you ought to consider such a father—
" even when dead—as a far greater benefit
" than a living father, such as most men are.

" You may think, perhaps, that there is no
" need for any one to tell you anything about
" one you knew so well. But I have known
" him, in fact, longer than you, for years
" before you were at all of an age to appre-
" ciate him; and I have also known much
" more of *other* men, and therefore know
" wherein he was distinguished from them.
" His being your father, you know, was the
" appointment of Providence, and was to
" you merely good fortune; to me, our
" friendship was the result of deliberate
" *choice;* and my good fortune was only
" in having such a man cast in my
" way.

" Most children who have had what is
" called a religious education, have been
" placed, more or less, in danger to their
" faith, by seeing religion associated either
" with weak and contemptible superstition,
" or with gloomy austerity. The contempt
" or disgust thus generated are hard to be got
" over. But your father was a man who, I
" am confident, supported the wavering faith
" of many, through his high intellectual
" endowments.

" Many a one, I have no doubt, said to
" himself—not in so many words, but in
" feeling,—'It cannot be all a delusion, for
" ' I see a man of uncommonly strong sense
" ' heartily embracing it;' and, 'It cannot,
" ' in itself, be anything dismal; for here is
" ' a most sincere Christian enjoying life with
" ' more than common cheerfulness, and yet
" ' enjoying it like a traveller on business,
" ' who admires every fine prospect, and
" ' enjoys the company of every pleasant
" ' fellow-traveller, yet never, for a moment,
" ' forgets his journey's end.'

" You should remark, also, the union in
" so many points of qualities which are apt
" to be considered as incompatible. In the
" bosom of his family *you* know what he
" was ;—a stranger might have thought him
" a man who had no heart but for his
" family. To a friend, *I* know what he was ;
" —a more zealous, affectionate, and constant
" friend, could not be found among those
" who have no relations at all. To the
" Church, to his country, to mankind at
" large, he was as full of public spirit and
" benevolence, as if he had neither friend

" nor relative in the world.   *   *   *   *   *

" ' BE YE WISE AS SERPENTS, AND HARMLESS
" ' AS DOVES,' is a precept for the union of
" qualities, as dissimilar as any can be that
" are not incompatible: and his life was a
" continual illustration of that text.   No
" child could be more guileless and full of
" simplicity of *heart;* no wily politician could
" be more cautiously and vigilantly exempt
" from simplicity of *head.*   Whether you will
" ever attain to an equality—or approach to
" equality—with him in ability, is a matter
" which does not principally depend on your-
" selves.   He was, in my opinion, most
" rarely gifted with a great variety of mental
" powers; but he was not the man who, if
" he had had but *one* talent, would have ' hid
" ' it in a napkin.'   He set himself in earnest
" to *regulate* his mind on Christian principles,
" and to make the best use he could of
" *all* the gifts, all the opportunities that he
" possessed.   This *you* can do, if you act
" upon the *impulse* of the moment, and not
" on *system*—on principle—according to the
" *best* judgment you can form of Christianity,
" and if you suffer your religion to evaporate

" in feelings and strong expressions instead
" of applying it steadily to the every-day
" business of life,—you will differ widely from
" him, not in the *number* of talents intrusted
" to you, but in the *use* of them.

" If you imitate, in this and in other points,
" the example he has left you, you will not
" only be doing what he would most earnestly
" wish you to do, but you will be preparing
" for a reunion with him ; for, as far as one
" can venture to speak confidently, one fal-
" lible mortal of another, I do feel confident,
" that if there be a heaven, there we shall
" find him, if the fault be not *ours*—

" ' Veniet felicius ævum,
" Quando iterum tecum, sim modo dignus, ero.'

" Think, my dear Charles, what would
" have been your delight at the unexpected
" recovery of your father, after the physicians
" had given him over. And yet, though
" restored to you for the present, death must
" ere long have parted you. But to meet
" such a friend, NEVER to part more. Oh,
" what would one not go through for that !

" We have only to go through a *life* like

" his.   God bless you and me to do this, is
" the sincere and fervent prayer of your
" faithful friend,

"RICHARD DUBLIN."

Dr. Dickinson had distinguished himself
in helping to promote Catholic Emancipation,
and other liberal measures; and the see of
Meath was offered to him by Lord Morpeth,*
then Chief Secretary for Ireland, "on ac-
" count of the high opinion the Government
" had formed of his character and prin-
" ciples;" and accompanied by an expression
of high personal gratification, as the appointment had been one which the noble Lord
had, for a long time, desired.   It was erroneously alleged, and is still rather generally
believed, that Dr. Whately had, as a matter
of course, exerted his influence with the
Government to procure the preferment of his
favourite secretary and chaplain; but we
have it on the authority of Dr. West, that
such a supposition is entirely destitute of
foundation, "as it had always been to him a
" point of scruple never to offer himself as

* Now Earl of Carlisle, Lord Lieutenant of Ireland.

" a debtor to any Government by asking
" favours either for himself or his friends."
There can be no doubt, however, that,
although not expressly avowed, Dr. Dickinson's elevation was effected mainly with a
view to compliment Dr. Whately.

Previous to obtaining the see, Dr. Dickinson had been appointed by Dr. Whately vicar
of St. Ann's, Dublin, in succession to Lord
Harburton, under whose incumbency an
incident occurred too amusing to omit from
these pages. Lord M——, as we are informed by Mr. Daunt, had obtained his title,
during a venal period, in gracious recognition
of some dexterous traffic in parliamentary
votes; and he was as unprincipled in pecu-
niary as in political transactions. When
Lord Kerry's house in Stephen's Green was
for sale, a Mrs. Keating ambitioned to become the possessor of a pew attached to it,
which she erroneously assumed belonged to
Lord M——, and waited upon him to nego-
tiate a purchase.

" I am not aware that I own any pew in
" St. Ann's," said Lord M——. " Pardon
" me," replied Mrs. Keating, " I find your

" Lordship has one ; and, if you have no ob-
" jection, I am willing to buy it."

Thus appealed to, Lord M—— threw out
no further obstacle. A bargain was struck ;
he took the money ; and on the following
Sunday Mrs. Keating, in an imposing suit of
rustling bombazine, sailed up the nave to take
possession of her pew ; but the beadle, with
much firmness, interposed, and, in reply to
her explanatory remonstrances, declared that
it was " the Kerry pew," and had never, at
any period, belonged to Lord M——.

The lady, smarting under the combined consciousness of the trick and the slight, retired
with considerably less inflation than she had
advanced, and lost no time in waiting on Lord
M——, in the hope of obtaining some redress.

" My Lord," she began, " as regards the
" pew at St. Ann's,"—

" Oh," interrupted the peer, laughing,
" you may have twenty more pews on the
" same terms."

" Pray don't add insult to injury, my
" Lord ; you must be aware of your mistake,
" and that you really never held any pew in
" St. Ann's."

"I told you so in the first instance," replied Lord M——.

"Under all the circumstances," proceeded his fair visitor, "I trust your Lordship will "kindly refund the money."

"Impossible, my dear madam; it's gone "long ago."

"But your Lordship's character"—

"That is also gone," exclaimed Lord M——, leaning back in his easy chair and laughing immoderately.

The money was never returned, and Lord M—— subsequently obtained an unenviable notoriety for selling the commissions of a regiment of militia in which he was colonel; and when upbraided with the act by the Lord Lieutenant, coolly replied, "Your Excellency "always told us to assimilate the militia as "far as possible to the line. In the line, "commissions are sold."

But we must again leave the cap and bells for the mitre. Those who admired Bishop Dickinson were very anxious that Dr. Whately should write his life. The following is his Grace's reply to Dr. West on the subject:—

" As for me, you cannot doubt that the
" idea of writing the memoir myself was very
" long, and certainly revolved in my own
" mind, and discussed with several friends;
" and I have long been fully satisfied that
" whatever I may write on that subject must
" not appear but as a posthumous work. I
" am, on the whole, perhaps, the best quali-
" fied of all to state the most important
" occurrences, and describe the most im-
" portant points of character, supposing me
" to be writing what is not to be read in my
" lifetime ; for that which is, I should be one
" of the worst qualified, from the very same
" causes, in a great measure; viz., my being
" *myself* so *mixed up* with him, that I could
" not (in an immediate publication) say, con-
" sistently with delicacy, even what many
" others, or almost any one else could. It is
" precisely because, as you say, I dug the
" diamond up, and set it, and wore it myself,
" that it would be unbearable for me to de-
" scribe and particularize, even as others
" could. In a posthumous work, great allow-
" ances are made. The indelicacy of egotism
" is pardoned in a dead man ; and so is a good

" deal of free stricture on others. Death
" gives a solemnity to what a man writes,
" knowing it is not to be seen till he is dead;
" and, moreover, people have nothing *more*
" to fear from him. In short, though the
" ' Palace of Truth' (of Madame Genlis) would
" be an intolerable place to *live* in, most
" would deem it a very good place to *die* in,
" *i. e.*, for the dying man to speak his mind
" quite freely about himself and others, once
" for all. So do not think of me, unless it
" be to ascertain any fact or date."

In June, 1845, Dr. Whately published
another enlarged edition of his " Thoughts
" on the Sabbath." From a copy now before
us, privately annotated in the autograph of
Dr. Whately, we find that the Rev. Dr.
Fitzgerald, his domestic chaplain and secretary, and now Bishop of Killaloe, who is
generally thought to have gone with his chief
on all points, and particularly on this vexed
question, holds an opposite policy. In the
published copy, Dr. Fitzgerald's name is not
given.

" According to the principles, therefore,
" which I have laid down in the essay ' On

" ' the Love of Truth,' " writes Whately, " I
" cannot allow myself even to deliberate as
" to the expediency of such a procedure.
" Yet a person of undoubted piety, well in-
" formed, and singularly intelligent, avowed
" to me, that though in his own mind he fully
" concurred with my opinion, he should yet,
" if he had the regulation of a Christian com-
" munity, think it advisable to inculcate on
" the mass of the people the strictest sabba-
" tarianism, based on the obligation of the
" Mosaic Law."—P. 24.

And again, 7 pages farther on, he writes :—

" I may add, that a very learned and intel-
" ligent friend of mine, having expressed his
" dissent from my views on this subject,
" I requested him, previously to this republi-
" cation of them, to let me know if there
" were any arguments that had weight with
" him, which I had overlooked, that I might
" be enabled either to correct my opinions,
" if erroneous, or to reply to objections
" against them. He did not, however, furnish
" me with anything whatever of the kind."

Every new edition of these " Thoughts on
" the Sabbath "—five appeared, and the Arch-

bishop was specially proud of them—sank
him deeper in the estimation of the Evangelical portion of his priests and flock. One
sustaining address on the subject, signed by
an archdeacon and a large share of the more
liberal clergy, did appear. A word of kindly
praise from any part of his diocese was such
a novelty, that Dr. Whately felt, on this occasion, deeply grateful; the writer was made
Bishop of Meath—and his sons received rich
livings from the Archbishop's hands.

The italicised portion of the following
note is in the autograph of Dr. Whately, and
belongs to the privately annotated volume, of
which we have had the use.

" I feel it right to add, that my lamented
" friend, Bishop Dickinson, whose ' Remains '
" have been recently published, was, as I
" learned subsequently, the person who drew
" up the above address ; and that he had
" always maintained the same doctrines with
" myself respecting the Sabbath and the Lord's
" day ; *and therefore I thought proper to bestow*
" *upon his son** *the parish of St. Anne's, not-*

* The Rev. Hercules H. Dickinson.

" *withstanding his youth and the number of*
" *clergy in my diocese of longer standing.*

" RD. DUBLIN."

In the Session of 1845, we find Dr.
Whately, in the House of Lords, eloquently
supporting, both by voice and vote, the Duke
of Wellington's motion in favour of the grant
to Maynooth College. And here again we
are forcibly reminded of the contrast between
Dr. Whately's policy and that of his predecessor, Dr. Magee, who, in his Parliamentary
evidence, recorded the opinion, that " the
" Maynooth Institution was not favourable to
" tranquillity, nor, I fear, to the principles of a
" sound civil allegiance." " Having," added
Dr. Magee, " given my opinion so decidedly
" on the Maynooth College, I beg leave to
" add, that at the time when that college was
" founded I felt the danger of an exclusive
" establishment for Roman Catholic students
" so strongly, that I then expressed my
" objections to it openly, and interested my-
" self as far as I properly could against it ;
" having urged to the representatives of the
" University of Dublin, of which I was then a
" member, the propriety of opposing the Bill

" for founding that college in its passage
" through Parliament."*

Dr. Whately, as usual, pursued the opposite direction in the very cathedral wherein
Dr. Magee said that the Catholics had a
" Church without a religion," and denounced
a monastic system of education. His successor, in 1845, delivered a Charge which
strongly condemned the opposition to Maynooth, adding, "that party spirit and political
" animosity was as bad as the worship of
" the grim and bloody Moloch, and the other
" abominations of the heathen. He could
" not ' see how a man who would not adopt
" ' a policy of expediency could sit in Parlia-
" ' ment at all.' ' Would they turn out Popery
" ' as Ferdinand and Isabella turned the Moors
" ' out of Spain ? ' He might be asked," he
said, " whether he considered religious error
" less an evil than a deficiency in gentlemanly
" habits and the polish of civilization ? The
" answer was obvious. The State might
" remedy the latter; it could not alter the

* " The Evidence of His Grace the Archbishop of
" Dublin [Dr. Magee] before the Select Committee of the
" House of Lords," pp. 119, 120,

" former evil. He denounced that dulness
" of thought, the result of an ill-conducted
" education, which confounded liberal tolera-
" tion with latitudinarian indifference."

This Charge, as may be readily believed,
elicited a renewed outburst of the storm
which had so long and so violently pursued
him in Ireland.

But Dr. Whately, although he voted on
the Maynooth question, never gave in Parliament what is called "a ministerial vote," nor
did he ever give even an election vote, if we
except his memorable support of Sir Robert
Peel on the Catholic question. He often
said that an ecclesiastic should constantly
aim never to incur the imputation of being a
party man.

Dr. Whately belonged to neither the High
nor the Low Church parties, but steadily
steered an even middle course.

In a fireside argument on toleration one
evening at his own house, Dr. Whately was
asked if he would not give some advantage
to those who were in the right over those
who were in the wrong? "By all means!"
replied the Archbishop, "but who are they?

"Of course we are right and the Romanists
"wrong?" proceeded the reluctant tolerator.
"I believe that I am right," said the Archbishop, "but I am not infallible: if you were
"to ask my friend Archbishop Murray if he
"was in the right, he would doubtless reply
"with more confidence in the affirmative;
"such is the advantage which the Roman
"Catholics have over us in possessing an
"infallible guide."

"But we have an infallible guide," remarked the other.

"In what?" asked Dr. Whately.

"In the Holy Scriptures," replied his companion.

"I grant that they are infallible," he went
on, "but how are you infallibly certain that
"you infallibly appreciate the infallible sense
"of the Holy Scriptures?"

His companion was silent.

"Observe," he continued, as he followed
up his advantage, "observe how Erasmus,
"Calvin, Socinus, and a host of other able
"men, all deduce different meanings from the
"same passage. Among the German Re-
"formers there was a complete recrimination

" on the grounds of mistranslation and mis-
" representation of the Bible.   Luther ac-
" cused Munzer with distorting the Word of
" God; and the same charge was laid at
" Luther's door by Zwinglius.   The transla-
" tion by Œcolampadius was severely criticised
" by Beza, whose version was in turn cen-
" sured by Castalio; and both Beza and Cas-
" talio were stigmatized by Molinceus as
" blundering translators."*

This conversation led to an elaborate train
of thought, which resulted in the publication
of " A Discourse on Infallibility," preached as
an ordination sermon in 1846.

In this performance Dr. Whately unfolded
all the resources of his powerful logical acumen, and in private conversation he was heard
to say "that a Protestant controversialist,

---

* The monstrous misinterpretation of the Old Testament by the Jews, as evinced in their misapprehension
and murder of the Messiah, shows how a vast people,
numbering many men of great learning, may all read
Holy Writ, and yet fail to appreciate its sense.   And it
is very remarkable, that after having crucified the real
Messiah they should have allowed themselves to be
duped by eighteen false Messiahs, of whom Zabbathai
Zevi was the last.—ED.

" who was victorious in other points but
" failed in this, was like a chess-player, who,
" after taking several pieces, is checkmated
" by the scholar's move."

The late Rev. Dr. O'Connell, the most
prominent Roman Catholic controversialist
of his day, regarding this discourse as an
assault on the Church of which he was a
member, replied to it from the pulpit at great
length, and subsequently published the sermon. Dr. Whately, however, in a letter to J. R.
Corballis, Esq., distinctly asserts that he did
not mean his Discourse on Infallibility as
an *attack* on any particular church, dashing
his pen under the word thus italicised.

The Directors of the Manchester Athenæum,
in October, 1846, invited a number of distinguished men, including the Archbishop of
Dublin and Lord Morpeth (now Earl of Carlisle), to enliven by their presence a breakfast
and soirée, with which the Institute was in-
augurated. Dr. Whately spoke with his accustomed originality and pith. At the breakfast
he said, among other good things,—

" It may be quite superfluous in me to de-
" tain you with any expression of my hearty

" sympathy and warm good wishes towards
" this place and Institution, because the very
" circumstance of my being here expresses
" that sufficiently (cheers). I certainly should
" not have left the very numerous and press-
" ing calls that I have in Dublin, overbur-
" dened as I generally am with business, to
" come over here for the sake of looking at
" a mere raree-show, or to attend a dance
" (cheers). I thought it incumbent on me to
" show the very great interest I have in every-
" thing concerning the diffusion of know-
" ledge (cheers). I feel, of course, great
" interest in the diffusion of knowledge every-
" where. I need not, however, say anything
" about that, because my life, in fact, has
" been occupied in official and non-official
" efforts of that kind. But I think that edu-
" cation is more peculiarly important in a
" wealthy and populous manufacturing town
" like this ; and I must say, though it may
" not be the warmest kind of panegyric, but
" it was what strikes me, that not only does
" this Institution do credit to the town of
" Manchester, but the want of it previously
" did the town great discredit."

The Archbishop was in still better humour at the soirée.

" I presume that those who have done me " the honour of calling upon me to address " some observations to you this evening, " have done so from the thought, perhaps, " that I should have to communicate to you " some of the results and observations ema- " nating from my own experience. I shall " do so, but very briefly, begging you, in the " first place, to bear in mind, that when I " said I had been for thirty-eight years " connected with education, I did not mean " that I had been occupied in making speeches " upon it. (Laughter.) I have been en- " gaged in the practice of it and not in " haranguing upon it; and, therefore, it is " not to be expected that I can address you " with the same eloquence that others can " do who have not seen and done as much as " I have. (Laughter and cheers.)"

Dr. Whately spoke at considerable length; but the effect was, perhaps, marred by bestriding his great hobby-horse of Irish national education, and giving it enormous rein.

" I would not hear this Manchester Insti-
" tution assailed with any calumny in Ireland
" or elsewhere, when it was in my power to
" repel it. (Cheers.) And I believe that
" none of you would willingly listen to any
" calumny that tended to disparage the
" merits or to defeat the object of such an
" institution as ours [that of National Educa-
" tion]. Gentlemen, it is not a Godless
" system "— and the Archbishop then entered upon an elaborate vindication of it. He
referred to the formidable antagonism with
which its earlier career was beset, and
exulted with no ordinary enthusiasm in the
triumphant success and firm footing which he
too hastily believed it had at last attained.

" A time for everything and everything in
" its proper place " was one of the aphoristic
copy-heads supplied by Dr. Whately for the
use of the children of the National School;
and favourite Scripture texts with him were
those occurring in the third chapter of Eccle-
siastes, beginning " All things have their
" season . . . . . A time to weep, and a time
" to laugh. A time to mourn, and a time
" to dance."

It cannot be said that he failed to practise
what he preached. In his principles and
movements he was methodical; and he
carried them out with an energetic tread
which often crushed the toes of those who
placed themselves in his way. He did not
like to see a man turning up the whites of
his eyes during dinner or other social hours;
and when the Bishop of O——, one day at
his own table, was descanting in a tone more
suitable to a Prie Dieu than the easy chair
in which he sat, Dr. Whately, dropping his
knife and fork, suddenly exclaimed, " Do
" you know the best way of dressing cab-
" bage ?" and, without waiting for a reply,
entered into an elaborate and instructive
detail regarding its culture, from the sowing
of the seed to the culinary preparation of the
plant.

CHAPTER II.

Dr. Whately was accustomed to receive
every Wednesday such of his clergy as chose
to frequent those levees. At first they were
very scantily attended; but as soon as the
report spread that as much wit as wisdom
characterized them, a push and a shove were
often needed to get in.

" The conferences " which took place on
these occasions were a rare treat to witness.
Conundrums and canons, logic and laughter,
puns and parables, fell from the Archbishop
in exhaustless profusion; wearing the mitre
one minute, donning the cap and bells the
next, but always wise and witty. Anon he
would be found " discoursing on some theo-
" logical point," writes his chaplain, Dr.
H. H. Dickinson, " throwing out hints for
" sermons, enlivening his remarks often by

" some fact of natural history, some curious
" illustration, or entertaining anecdote, under
" the guise of pleasantry almost always
" impressing some important truth. There
" was an occasional abrupt unceremonious-
" ness and inattention to superficial courte-
" sies, but the genuine kindliness of the man
" soon made those who were brought into
" more frequent intercourse with him un-
" mindful of these peculiarities of manner."

" The Archbishop's abrupt unceremonious-
" ness and inattention to superficial courte-
" sies," as noticed by his chaplain, struck
those against whom they jostled all the more
forcibly, from the fact that no one made less
allowance for the absence of courteous ceremony than Dr. Whately himself. In one of
his published works he lays down the principle with almost all the authority of an
article of faith.

" Mankind are not formed to live without
" ceremony and form : The ' inward, spiritual
" ' grace ' is very apt to be lost without the
" ' external, visible sign.' Many are con-
" tinually setting up for the expulsion of
" ceremonies from this or that, and often,

" with advantage, when *they* have so mul-
" tiplied as to grow burdensome ; but if ever
" they have carried this too far, they have
" been either forced to bring back some
" ceremonies, or have found the want of
" them. The same is found in the minor
" department of manners; when form is too
" much neglected, true politeness suffers
" diminution; then, we are obliged to bring
" some back, and when these again grow
" burdensome, we lay them aside again ; so
" that there is a continual flux and reflux.
" Upon the whole, we may conclude that
" *ceremony* and form of every kind derive
" their necessity from our imperfection. If
" we were perfectly spiritual, we might
" worship God without any form at all, with-
" out ever uttering words ; as we are not,
" it is a folly to say, ' One may be just as
" ' pious on one day as another, in one place or
" ' posture as another,' &c.; I answer, angels
" may; man cannot. Again, if we were all per-
" fectly benevolent, good-tempered, attentive
" to the gratifying of others, &c., we might
" dispense with all the forms of good-breed-
" ing; as it is, we cannot; we are not

" enough of heroes to fight without disci-
" pline. Selfishness will be sure to assail us
" if we once let the barriers be broken down.
" At the same time it is evident from what
" has been said that the *higher our nature is*
" *carried, the less form we need.*

" But though we may deservedly congra-
" tulate society on being able to dispense
" with this or that ceremony, do not let us
" be in a hurry to do so, till we are sure
" we *can* do without it. It is taking away
" crutches to cure the gout. The opposite
" extreme of substituting the external form
" for the thing signified, is not more danger-
" ous or more common, than the neglect of
" that form. It is all very well to say,
" ' There is no use in bidding good-morrow
" ' or good-night to those who know I wish
" ' it ; of sending one's love, in a letter, to
" ' those who do not doubt it,' &c. All this
" is very well in theory, but it will not do
" for practice. Scarce any friendship, or any
" politeness, is so strong as to be able to
" subsist without any external supports of
" this kind ; and it is even better to have too
" much form than too little."

True to this principle, Richard Whately kept up an uninterrupted correspondence with his old friends. " Correspondences," says Sydney Smith, who was never known to preserve a letter, " correspondences are like " small-clothes before the invention of sus- " penders—it is impossible to keep them up." The task was not difficult to Dr. Whately, who used to say that letters were the rivets of friendship. The following is addressed to his old preceptor, Bishop Copleston, and appears in the life of that prelate :—

" DUBLIN, 7th July, 1845.
    " MY DEAR LORD,—
    " I am bound to send, and you to receive, " as a kind of lord of the soil, every production " of my pen, as a token of acknowledgment " that from you I have derived the main " principles on which I have acted and " speculated through life. Not that I have " adopted anything from you implicitly and " on authority, but from conviction, pro- " duced by the reasons you adduced. This, " however, rather increases the obligation, " since you furnished me not only with the

" theorems, but the demonstrations — not
" only with the fruit, but the trees that bore
" them. It cannot, indeed, be proved that
" I should not have embraced the very same
" principles if I had never known you ; and,
" in like manner, no one can prove that the
" battle of Waterloo would not have been
" fought and won if the Duke of Wellington
" had been killed the day before, but still
" the fact remains that the duke did actually
" gain that battle. And it is no less a fact
" that my principles were learnt from you.
" When it happens that we completely concur
" as to the application of any principle, it is
" so much the more agreeable ; but in all cases
" the law remains in force, that ' whatsoever
" ' a man soweth, that also shall he reap ;'
" and the credit, or the discredit, of having
" myself to reckon among your works, must,
" in justice, appertain to you.

" Believe me to be, at the end of forty
" years, your grateful and affectionate friend
" and pupil,

" R. DUBLIN."

" I have often said," writes Moore, " that
" correspondence between friends should be

" like the flow of notes in music—if too
" long an interval is allowed to take place
" between the tones, one loses the chain of
" song, the idea of melody is interrupted,
" and we listen to the sounding note (when
" it comes) with faint, or at least, diminished
" gratification." Whately felt this, and acted
accordingly.

Nor did he belong to that class who,
when a friend dies, consign his memory to
oblivion. His Charge, delivered in 1850, is
dedicated to the revered memory of Edward
Copleston, " with affectionate and sorrowing
" veneration."

It was often made a source of complaint
or reproach against Dr. Whately, that he
cultivated few friendships, and enclosed his
existence within a narrow circle. Of the great
bulk of his species, it must be confessed he
had no very exalted opinion. " The gene-
" rality of mankind," he would say, " are as
" good and as wise as — the generality."
One circumstance might be told, which
throws light on the motives which greatly
influenced Dr. Whately in his choice of
friends.

" I see no reason," he said, " why those " who *have been* dearest friends on earth, " should not, when admitted to the future " happy state, continue to be so, with full " knowledge and recollection of their former " friendship. If a man is still to continue " (as there is every reason to suppose) a " social being, and *capable* of friendship, it " seems contrary to all probability that he " should cast off or forget his former friends, " who are partakers with him of the like " exaltation. He will indeed be greatly " changed from what he was on earth, and " unfitted perhaps for friendship with such " a being as one of us is *now;* but his friend " will have undergone, by supposition, a ' corresponding change."

The Irish famine, and the pestilential cycles which it left behind, elicited from Dr. Whately a remarkable Charge. Addressing the Protestant clergy " on the right use of national afflictions," he urged them to alleviate the sufferings of the famine-stricken poor—not to ask if the applicant were a Catholic or a Protestant, but rather to imitate the Samaritan, who inquired not whether the wounded traveller was a worshipper at Jerusalem or at Mount Gerizim. The Archbishop praised the clergy for having thus acted so far—" a " testimony," he added, " whatever may be " its value in other respects, is at least that " of one whom you know by experience— " some of you by very long experience—to be " incapable of courting popularity by speaking " otherwise than he really thinks."

The system of proselytizing by means of breakfasts and breeches, to which more than one evangelical bishop notoriously lent his sanction, received caustic condemnation from Dr. Whately in this Charge.

" Attempts were made indeed, he said, in " some few instances (as I remarked to you " last year) to induce persons to carry on a " system of covert proselytism by holding " out relief to bodily wants and sufferings as " a kind of bribe for conversion,"—but " these " attempts," he added, " were almost inva- " riably unsuccessful." And again :—

" While it is our duty to take every suit- " able occasion of promulgating and ad- " vocating—mildly indeed, but boldly and " firmly—what we deliberately believe to be

" revealed truth and refuting error, it is both
" unsuitable and injurious to the cause of
" truth generally, and to gospel truth more
" especially, to appeal to interested motives
" in that cause, to endeavour by such influ-
" ence either to bias men's minds, or to extort
" from them hypocritical professions. Truth
" should indeed be earnestly recommended,
" but recommended as truth; and error
" censured because it is error, without any
" appeal to men's temporal wants, and
" sufferings, and interests, or to any other
" such motives as ought not in such a question
" to be allowed to operate.

" In the words of my lamented friend Dr.
" Arnold, words as true and as important
" to be laid to heart as ever were penned by
" uninspired man—the *highest truth, if pro-*
" *fessed by any one who believes it not in his*
" *heart, is, to him, a lie,* and he sins greatly
" by professing it. Let us try as much as
" we will to convince our neighbours, but let
" us *beware of influencing their conduct when*
" *we fail in influencing their convictions.** He

---

* The italics are Dr. Whately's.

" who bribes or frightens his neighbour into
" doing an act which no good man would do
" for reward, or from fear, is tempting his
" neighbour to sin ; he is assisting to lower
" and harden his conscience—to make him
" act for the favour or from the fear of man
" instead of for the favour or from the fear
" of God; and if this be a sin in him, it is a
" double sin in us to tempt him to it."

Dr. Whately referred to the Young Ireland movement, which, goaded rather than checked by the decimation of the bone and sinew of the country, had assumed in 1848, under the leadership of W. Smith O'Brien and others, at first a strongly seditious, and later, a boldly revolutionary tone. The pregnancy of recent events he compared to the pestilence " mentioned by Thucydides, which " introduced a general lawlessness."

It was a mistake, he contended, to assume that the usual and natural effect of affliction was improving to the moral character. " All " things, it is true, work together for good " to them that love God ; but it is to such " only," he added, with mingled humour and bitterness, " that this good can be confidently " promised."

The Judicial and Episcopal Bench of Dublin were about this time brought into collision by a charge from the late Chief Justice Doherty, in which he regretted that Dr. Whately should have allowed a scandal connected with one of his clergy to come before the public in a court of law instead of having privately investigated it in the archiepiscopal study.

A long letter from the Archbishop in reply gave the Chief Justice a Roland for his Oliver.

From Dr. Whately's antecedents, it may well be supposed that to the Irish Confederation of 1847-8, he placed himself in an antagonism much more determined than that which had previously indirectly teased the Repeal Association. At a meeting of the Dublin Statistical Society held on June 19th, 1848, a moment when all Ireland was drilling, and Dublin seemed like a slumbering volcano, the Archbishop propounded a panacea against the threatened siege, which strongly suggested the old joke of "Nothing like "leather"!

" He spoke of calling forth the genius of " the people in the direction of Political

" Economy, not only to have it cultivated
" among the learned, but also amongst the
" people generally, as the only means which
" existed of rescuing the country from con-
" vulsion. It was a mistake to suppose that
" religion or morals alone would be sufficient
" to save a people from revolution. No;
" they would not be sufficient, if a proper
" idea of Political Economy was not cultivated
" by that people. A man, even of the purest
" mind and most exalted feelings, without a
" knowledge of Political Economy, could not
" be secured from being made instrumental
" in forwarding most destructive and dis-
" astrous revolutions. A man of that kind
" might think it possible for the landlords to
" support and feed all the poor of the country;
" he might adopt the doctrine, that a landlord
" with a limited number of acres should sup-
" port and feed an unlimited number of
" mouths. Should that doctrine be adopted,
" and laws passed to that effect, the landlords
" would be crushed by that ruinous system,
" and swept off as a class altogether. A man
" of this kind, though of the purest feelings
" and intentions, and of the most exalted

" morality, may be led to undertake the for-
" mation of what is called a 'provision-*all*'
" government—(laughter)—and then a ten
" hours' labour bill would be brought in;
" then it would be reduced to a working
" time of eight hours, six hours, and so on—
" doubtless very popular, till labour and in-
" dustry would be at a stand; and a people
" led by such men would fall into the wildest
" excesses, and would take part in any ruin-
" ous revolution fatal to all classes, and not
" the least fatal to the working classes them-
" selves."

" The study of Political Economy," he
went on to say, " was one particularly im-
" portant in a free country, where every one
" might be said to take part in the govern-
" ment of the state—and he had heard so
" much about the enslavement of Ireland,
" that he was thereby convinced she was a
" free country. At all times, and especially
" in troubled times like the present, a
" knowledge of the principles of this science
" was essential to the prosperity of the
" nation. Everything turned upon sound
" and just views of what were the proper

" functions of the government, and what
" effects the interference of government could
" produce on the prosperity of the country.
" That was especially to be considered at the
" present time, when there was so much of
" popular excitement; because on this sub-
" ject, as on most others, the fallacies lay
" upon the surface. He who would look for
" pearls must dive deeply. It had been well
" remarked by Hooker, that if a man haran-
" gued a multitude in order to prove to them
" that they were not well governed, he would
" never want hearers. But if they did not
" teach the principles of Political Economy,
" they would allow the land to remain fallow,
" and weeds would spring up of themselves.
" For example, what could seem more obvious
" to an ignorant or uninstructed multitude,
" than if it were said to them: 'What a
" 'shame it is that there should be a man
" 'having £5,000 a year, when hundreds are
" 'starving. If that sum were divided
" 'amongst one hundred poor families, it
" 'would give them £50 a year each, and
" 'by carrying out that principle gene-
" 'rally, we would have no poor.' Now, it

" could be easily explained to them, that this
" wealth *was* in reality divided, and that rich
" men did in reality support poor families by
" affording them profitable employment. It
" could be shown that if we plundered all
" the rich, and distributed their wealth
" amongst the poor, instead of benefiting the
" labouring classes thereby, we should render
" property insecure, and destroy all incen-
" tives to honourable industry."

John Mitchell had, previously to this
speech, attacked Dr. Whately very pointedly
in the *United Irishman* newspaper. He declared that the Archbishop's principle was
" England for the English, Scotland for the
" Scotch," and " Ireland, not for the Irish,"
but " for everybody," else what brought him
here? He was of opinion that if the office
were open to competition numbers would be
found to discharge the duties in all respects
as efficiently for £800 a year!

Dr. Whately took no direct notice of his
assailant, but proceeded to urge Young Ireland to think more of potato-drills than
of drilling; and instead of turning their
thoughts to democratic politics, to study

political economy. He contended that these principles could be explained even to the ploughman, and made clear to the comprehension of children.

" If I had broached the idea some years " ago," he said, " that it was possible to " instruct children in the science of Political " Economy, it would have been laughed at " as the most chimerical notion that could " enter into the brain of a visionary. But " instead of *saying* that such a thing was " possible, I tried the experiment; and it " fully succeeded. There were certain " familiar treatises on this subject, con- " taining the fundamental principles of the " science, which were now placed in the " hands of a large portion of the popu- " lation of Great Britain and Ireland, " and were taught in more than 4,000 " schools to the children of the poorer " classes in this country; and on examina- " tion it would be found that the boys who " formed the higher classes in these schools " —lads of from thirteen to fourteen years " of age—had an intimate knowledge of the " principles of this science, which was gene-

" rally considered to be so abstruse and " difficult of attainment."

The Archbishop, finding that the peasantry regarded his proffered principles of Political Economy with indifference, again lost temper, and declared that he could hardly wonder at this proceeding on the part of the illiterate multitude when Trinity College, Dublin, had viewed Political Economy with such incredible ignorance and apathy, that it proved a herculean labour to make them appreciate and adopt it.

His Grace proceeded, as opportunity offered, to combat the prejudices against the study, and especially those which represent it as unfavourable to religion.

" Next to sound religion, sound Political " Economy was most essential to the well- " being of society. It had been too much " the practice, heretofore, to confine this " species of knowledge to a few; and the " object of the Statistical Society was to " diffuse it as widely as possible amongst the " people. When any one spoke to him of the " dangers attending the study of Political " Economy, he would reply:—' Undoubtedly

" 'the dangers are great, but the way to
" ' avoid them is to substitute sound doc-
" 'trines for fallacies; for one or the other
" ' you must have.' "

Probably enough has been said of the
power of Whately's intellect, which all the
world knows was one of no ordinary calibre.
But as the munificence of his charity is comparatively unknown, it may both " point a
" moral, and adorn our tale," to cite some
authenticated illustrations of it. His generous disbursements are all the more remarkable from the ardour with which he always
inculcated principles of economy.   One of
the copy heads supplied by him to the children of the national schools is, " A penny
" saved is a penny gained."

Dr. Whately's charity was further the more
striking from the strangely stern pertinacity
with which he always laboured to disprove
the merit of " good works." In his " Les-
" sons on Morals," vi. sect. 5, he says that
inasmuch as it is the duty of all to be good
—a debt which we are bound to discharge—
nobody can be justly entitled to reward for
merely paying his debts : but " If a man

"*fail* to pay what he is bound to pay, he is
" liable to punishment. If he does pay his
" debts, he is exempt from punishment ; and
" that is all he can claim."

A clergyman, who made a touching appeal to his generosity, was unhesitatingly
accommodated with a loan of £400. He
deserted the Archbishop's levees, and was
not seen at the Palace, or heard of, for many
years after. One day Dr. Whately's study door
opened noiselessly, and the borrower stood
before him, presenting an aspect half-sug-
gestive of Haydon's figure of Lazarus,
and half of the Prodigal Son's return.
" Hilloa !" exclaimed the Archbishop, start-
ing up to kill the fatted calf, " what in
" the name of wonder became of you so
" long ? "

" I did not like to present myself be-
" fore your Grace," replied the clergyman,
who was a man of high literary attainments,
and of higher principle, " until I found
" myself in a position to return the sum
" which you so generously lent me "—saying
which he advanced to the study table and
deposited upon it a pile of Bank notes.

" Tut, tut !" said the Archbishop, taking
the arm of his visitor, " put up your money,
" and now come down to luncheon."

A remark made by the late Sir Philip
Crampton, which sounded at the time extra-
vagant, will, now that Dr. Whately's charity
is better bruited, fail to awaken surprise.

At a meeting of the Irish Zoological Society, some years ago, when a subscription
among the members was on foot, Dr. ——
suggested that Dr. Whately's name ought to
be put down for at least £50.

" He has not got it," interposed Sir Philip
Crampton, " no one knows him better than
" I do ; he gives away every farthing of his
" income ; and so privately is it bestowed
" that the recipients themselves are the only
" witnesses of his bounty."

We are ourselves acquainted with some
remarkable instances of his generosity, for the
accuracy of which we can vouch. A ripe scholar
and gentleman died some years since in Dublin, leaving his family almost destitute. Dr.
Whately, having been made acquainted with
the circumstance, aided them by the munifi-
cent relief of £1,000. A classical teacher

was threatened by a legal execution; Mr.
M——, on his behalf, represented his painful
situation to the Archbishop, who, having
been informed that £250 would make him a
comparatively free and happy man, filled a
cheque for that amount, and thus averted the
catastrophe.

Mammon's throne was illy served when in
Archbishop Whately's presence. He weak-
ened its influence and grasp around rather
by the scorch of his caustic wit than by any
violent muscular effort to subvert the one or
unlock the other.

" Many a man," he said, " who may admit
" it to be impossible to serve God and Mam-
" mon at one and the same time, yet wishes
" to serve Mammon and God; first the one,
" as long as he is able; and then the other."

Dr. Whately's generosity to the needy was
not impulsive, but well regulated.

In the warmth of argument at a dinner
party, at Dr. Lloyd's, the following remark
was drawn from him :—" I have been Arch-
" bishop of Dublin for — years; I have given
" away upwards of £50,000 in charity; I have
" doubtless frequently erred; but there is

" one thing with which I cannot reproach
" myself—I never relieved a beggar in the
" streets.   I take care so to administer relief
" as not to encourage vice, or its mother,
" idleness."

To the poor of Stillorgan, however, Dr.
Whately and his wife were steady friends.
Every poor widow, irrespective of her creed,
had her weekly pension and bag of coal. Aptly
might the lines of Goldsmith be applied :—

" No surly porter stood in guilty state
" To spurn imploring famine from the gate."

When Dr. Whately gave away considerable
sums of money to relieve deserving persons
in temporary difficulties, he has sometimes
been known to get them to sign a document
promising to repay the amount whenever
able, not to himself but to persons circumstanced like those who had benefited by his
bounty.

Some of his views on the subject of charit-
able disbursement are extremely curious,
original, and occasionally contradictory.

" It is now generally acknowledged," he
said, " that relief afforded to want, as mere

" want, tends to increase that want; while
" the relief afforded to the sick, the infirm,
" and the disabled, has plainly no tendency
" to multiply its own objects. Now it is
" remarkable, that the Lord Jesus employed
" His miraculous power in healing the sick
" *continually*, but in feeding the hungry only
" twice; while the power of multiplying food
" which He then manifested, as well as His
" directing the disciples to take care and
" gather up the fragments that remained that
" nothing might be lost, served to mark that
" the abstaining from any like procedure on
" other occasions was deliberate design. In
" this, besides other objects, our Lord had
" probably in view to afford us some instruc-
" tion, from His example, as to the mode of
" our charity. Certain it is, that the reasons
" for this distinction are now, and ever must
" be, the same as at that time."

When the Social Inquiry Society, since
amalgamated with the Dublin Statistical
Society, was started, in 1850, Dr. Whately
evinced his interest in the application of
" scientific investigation to social questions."
He accepted the Presidency of the Society,

subscribed munificently to its funds, and delivered the address at its first annual meeting. "The great advantage of such a "Society," his Grace observed, "was that "they could deliberate on each subject "according to its own merits, and through "the means of the investigations which they "conducted, and the observations made as "to the result of them, they might so far "affect public opinion as to have ultimately "measures ready prepared with all that "discussion which Parliament could not and "would not afford to them, and thus the "foundations laid of such improvements in "their social condition, as they never could "expect from any parliament existing in a "free country, which would be always open "to the disadvantage of party contests for "power. He hoped their example would be "followed in other places,"* and "would feel

---

* The Society thus founded in Ireland, under the presidency of Archbishop Whately, for the scientific investigation of social questions, preceded by six years the Association for the Promotion of Social Science, which was founded under the presidency of Lord Brougham in 1856.

"it a very great triumph if this country
"should assert its equality, at least, with
"any other portion of the British empire,
"by setting an example which would here-
"after be followed by Great Britain."

In 1850, some symptoms of vacillation,
however guardedly covered, showed themselves in Dr. Whately's public policy. Dr.
Whately was too thorough an Englishman
not to participate in the contagious panic and
outburst of jealous feeling which swept the
length and breadth of England on the nomination by the Pope of a Catholic hierarchy
deriving territorial titles from English towns.
But he, nevertheless, more than hesitated to
support the Titles Bill, which forbade Catholic bishops, under penalties they could not
pay, and the non-payment of which would
doom them to prison, to acknowledge, even
to their own flocks, that they were the pastors
whom the Head of the Roman Catholic
Church, acting according to its known dis-
cipline, had placed over them.

After the Ecclesiastical Titles Bill had
passed, Dr. Whately published a Charge in
which he strongly condemned that oppressive

measure, but somewhat inconsistently insisted
that if it did become law, it should be applied
to Ireland as well as to England. He considered the Bill mischievous, and, contrary to
the general accuracy of his logical deductions,
he was anxious to extend the mischief as far
as possible. Lord Monteagle, on the other
hand, had from the beginning opposed every
part of the Bill; but, finding his opposition
ineffectual, he sought to confine within the
narrowest possible limits a measure fraught
with mischief. In a pointed pamphlet he
impaled the anomalous doctrine of the Archbishop. "Dr. Whately," he said, "had laid
" down the four following propositions : First,
" that the exemption from the Act would have
" been an abandonment of the royal preroga-
" tive in Ireland, while that prerogative
" required and received a parliamentary con-
" firmation in England; secondly, it would
" have been a virtual violation of the fifth
" article of the Union; thirdly, it would have
" been imputed not to justice, but to fear;
" and, fourthly, it would have been dangerous
" and dishonourable. To the first of these
" arguments Lord Monteagle urges that it was

" in England, not in Ireland, that the prero-
" gative was violated, and that it would
" have been enough to repel an aggression,
" without making an inconvenient declaration
" of abstract rights. Further, he observes
" that the measure is either too wide or too
" narrow—too wide for the purposes of re-
" taliation, too narrow for the declaration of
" the prerogative, in which case the colonies
" ought to have been included. As to the
" second point, Lord Monteagle showed the
" danger of teaching the Irish nation that
" the Act was extended to Ireland for the
" sake of the Established Church, intimating
" that the one may probably be considered
" as a poor equivalent for the other. It
" also appeared that on the introduction of
" the Tithe Commutation Act in 1823, Sir
" John Nicholl remarked on the difference
" between England and Ireland, and regretted
" that this contrast was not more strongly
" stated in the preamble of the bill, and the
" preamble was amended accordingly. So in
" the King's Speech in 1833 he is made to
" say, that though the Established Church of
" Ireland is by law permanently united with

" that of England, the peculiarities of their
" respective circumstances will require a sepa-
" rate consideration, and this sentiment was
" echoed by the House of Commons. Fur-
" ther, Lord Ashburton introduced his pro-
" position for substituting the congregational
" for the parochial system in Ireland, which
" would effectually have destroyed the iden-
" tity or even similarity of the two Churches,
" by the advice and at the suggestion of no
" less a person than the Archbishop of Dublin
" himself.　Other differences between the
" two Churches are, that the Church of Ire-
" land has no convocation, no *congé d'élire*,
" and no appeal in spiritual cases to the
" Privy Council. The Archbishop's third
" proposition is answered by the observation
" that we ought not to be prevented from
" doing what is just by the fear of having our
" motives misrepresented, and that the im-
" putation of fear is much more likely to
" attach to a government which forbears to
" prosecute than to one which refrains from
" legislating. The fourth proposition Lord
" Monteagle answered by historical proof of
" the existence of the Roman Catholic Church

" of Ireland from the time of the Reforma-
" tion." And in discharging this part of his
task some curious facts transpired. " I now
" refer to the authority of one whose name
" deserves veneration wherever the Christian
" faith extends,—I allude to the pious Bishop
" Bedell. He states to Archbishop Laud, in
" 1629, ' The Popish clergy is more numerous
" ' than we, *and in full exercise of all jurisdic-*
" ' *tion ecclesiastical by their vicars-general,*
" ' who are so confident that they excommu-
" ' nicate such as come to our courts. *The*
" ' *Primate* himself lives in my parish. The
" ' *Bishop* in another part of my diocese, a
" ' little further off. Each parish has a priest,
" ' and sometimes two or three apiece. In
" ' some cases mass is said in our churches.'
" The excellent Bedell seems to have felt no
" scruple in applying the title of Primate and
" Bishop to his Roman Catholic neighbours,
" nor does he seem, any more than his bro-
" thers of Derry, whose report we have cited,
" to have placed any reliance on those laws
" which, in the Royal Visitation, were de-
" clared to be ' powerless,' but which Sir F.
" Thesiger's amendments seek to revive, and

" to which he wishes ' to give a voice at the
" ' present time.'—(Debate, 28th June.) Mr.
" Justice Cressy, in the reign of Charles I.,
" fully confirms the preceding evidence of the
" Bishops.   Writing to the Lord Deputy, in
" 1633, he states officially : ' There is raised
" ' up a *Romish hierarchy* of bishops, vicars-
" ' general, &c., *to the overthrowing of the*
" ' *royal power.*'   In the same year Bishop
" Bedell writes to the Lord Deputy : ' The
" ' Pope hath *a clergy*, if I may guess from
" ' my own diocese, *double in number to ours,*
" ' and styling themselves in print, *Ego, Dei*
" ' *et Apostolicæ sedis gratiâ, Episcopus Fern-*
" ' *ensis, Ossoriensis,*' &c.   And in order to
" prove that there is nothing new under the
" sun, the Bishop adds : ' His Holyness *hath*
" ' *created a new University in Dublin to con-*
" ' *front with His Majesty's College there.*'   But
" further resemblance will be found to exist :
" Synods were held at Kells, Armagh, and
" Kilkenny.   In 1666, a national Synod was
" held, with *the connivance of the Government.*
" Peter Talbot, the Roman Catholic Arch-
" bishop of Dublin, *acted as Royal Commis-*
" *sioner.*   The offences of the Irish Govern-

" ment of Charles II. throw the imputed
" delinquencies of Lord Clarendon and the
" Colonial Secretary far into the shade.* We
" are told, that 'the Roman Catholic Arch-
" 'bishop was admitted to attend the Privy
" 'Council in his vestments ;' and to com-
" plete the whole, 'the Lord Lieutenant lent
" 'his official plate for the celebration of high
" 'mass !'"

Lord Monteagle proceeded to show Dr.
Whately that the Roman Catholic Establish-
ment had subsisted through the times of
Elizabeth, and was not affected by her Act of
Supremacy, survived the cruelties of Crom-
well, and the terrible severity of the Penal
Code. But the logical queries proposed by
Lord Monteagle were more to the Arch-

---

* Lord Monteagle doubtless alludes to a letter of the
Lord Lieutenant's, written in 1849, which addressed Dr.
Murray, the Catholic Archbishop of Dublin, as " My
" dear Lord." The second allusion is to a letter of Earl
Grey's in which the following passage occurs :—

" I have to instruct you hereafter officially to address
" the prelates of the Roman Catholic Church in your
" Government by the title of ' Your Grace,' or ' Your
" ' Lordship,' as the case may be.—EARL GREY, from
" Downing Street, *Nov.* 20, 1847."

bishop's humour, and adroitly paid his Grace in his own coin. Touching the threatened application of the Ecclesiastical Titles Bill to Ireland, to which the recent Papal rescript had made no reference, Lord Monteagle wittily said,—

" According to ordinary experience, the " application to those in health of a remedy " prescribed for the sick, is a startling novelty " in hospital practice. To compel me to " swallow cholera medicines, because my " neighbour is in the blue state of collapse, " does not seem very reconcilable with " common sense or discretion. But when " the question is, not the administration of a " remedy, but the application of a severe " punishment, I am at a loss to find either " a precedent, or an excuse, for so anoma- " lous a proceeding."

Second only in intensity to the outburst evoked by " the Papal Aggression," was the storm which, a short time previously, agitated the Evangelical Church of England and Ireland, by the appointment of Dr. Renn Dickson Hampden, Regius Professor of Divinity at Oxford, to the Bishopric of Hereford.

The late Archdeacon Strong, writing to Dr. Whately, notices " this manifestation so de-
" cided in its character, and so unusual.
" Being aware," he adds, " that your Grace's
" former connection with the University of
" Oxford has afforded you ample opportunity
" of being fully acquainted with the senti-
" ments of Dr. Hampden and with the cir-
" cumstances of the question generally, we
" respectfully beg leave to request that you
" will be so good as to favour us with your
" views on the various bearings of this im-
" portant subject."

Dr. Whately adopted the suggestion and published some " Statements and Reflec-
" tions " on the subject, which an influential Print stigmatized as " ill-tempered, bilious,
" and illogical." The latter epithet, how-ever, conveys less than his due, inasmuch as Whately showed the inconsistency of the remonstrants urging Ministers, on the very ground of Dr. Hampden's theological un-soundness, to leave him in the office of Regius Professor of Theology, whose duty it would be to train successive generations of Divinity students !

As to the tone of the pamphlet being "ill-
"tempered," it doubtless originated in some
personal feeling awakened by the resemblance
between the outcry against Dr. Hampden's
appointment to a see, and that which seven-
teen years previously greeted the elevation
of Whately. Hampden, like Whately, had
been Bampton Lecturer; they held many
views in common; and both possessed an
equal share of enemies. Moreover, they had
been intimately associated as college contemporaries; and for all such persons Dr.
Whately had a robust memory. It may with
truth be said that he never forgot a friend or
a fact.

Dr. Whately took as his text an article
from one of the leading journals, and with
much warmth impaled the views advanced.
His passion for punning peeps out drolly :—

"What in the name of common sense,"
says this writer, "could induce Lord John
"Russell to choose out Dr. Hampden, from
"among the 15,000 clergymen of the Church
"of England, to be the new Bishop of Here-
"ford? Dr. Hampden is *less than nobody*."

"The writer," interposes Whately, "evi-

" dently does not mean this to be understood
" as signifying that he is ' inferior to none.'
" He is the representative of NO PARTY.
" He is the mouthpiece of NO PARTICULAR SET
" OF OPINIONS. The Evangelicals distrust him
" to the full as much as the High Church
" party. His claims, considered as a private
" person, are *nil*. FAMILY INFLUENCE * he
" has none."

Dr. Whately in handling this paragraph
remarked that " all men of any generous
" feeling wish to distinguish a revered and
" deserving man who has been long subject
" to unjust and cruel persecution. As to
" his works," he said, " they had been tried
" in the fire. For eleven years they have
" been scrutinized with the utmost diligence,
" in search of something on which to fix a
" charge of heresy. They ' urged him ve-
" ' hemently, and provoked him to speak
" ' of many things; laying wait for him,
" ' and seeking to catch something out of
" ' his mouth, that they might accuse
" ' him.' For eleven years he has been

* These capitals are Dr. Whately's.

" demanding a regular trial, and courting
" investigation; and in all that time, nothing
" has been established against him. He
" has been assailed only by declamations, by
" rumours and suspicions, — and by gross
" falsifications. How many theological
" authors are there whose writings have un-
" dergone such a scrutiny? How many of
" his accusers are there whose own sermons
" could undergo such an ordeal? When,
" then, a man, otherwise judged to possess
" high claims, has had these claims thus
" strengthened, through the increased con-
" fidence justly felt in one whom his oppo-
" nents have long and earnestly, but
" vainly, endeavoured to convict of error,—
" to have passed over such a man would
" naturally and reasonably have been re-
" garded as a sacrifice to party prejudice,—
" as an indication of a base and cowardly
" dread of unjust clamour. A Minister who
" should so act would be considered—by the
" best men in his own times, and by almost
" all men in future times—as incurring de-
" served censure, for the sake of avoiding
" undeserved."

Though no charge of heresy was conclusively established against Dr. Hampden, yet a Convocation of the University of Oxford, in 1836, passed a vote of censure upon him. The legality of this vote, Dr. Whately considered doubtful, and, consequently, whether it is to be regarded as properly " the act " of the University," and he also alleged " that it was disregarded and virtually " repealed by the University itself."

" Dr. Hampden denied altogether the right " of Convocation to deprive the Regius Pro- " fessor of his seat at the Board which ap- " points Select Preachers. He is understood " to have consulted eminent legal advisers on " this point, and to have been confirmed in " his opinion by them. He is generally be- " lieved to have been deterred from following " up his claim in a court of justice merely by " his inability to meet the enormous and in- " deed ruinous expenses of such a procedure. " But he never ceased to protest solemnly " against the legality of that vote."

Dr. Whately opened this pamphlet in the old Paleyan fashion. " If we were to suppose " some intelligent and right-minded Church-

" man to have resided for the last fifteen
" years in some remote part, and to return
" to his country, he would be greatly asto-
" nished," &c. ; and ended by urging the
Remonstrants to take St. Paul's advice, and
" Mind their own business."

The evangelical Bishop of Winchester, and
the men whom he led, were mercilessly handled
in these " Statements and Reflections."

Dr. Whately took a leading part, about
this time, in addressing a letter of protest to
the Archbishop of Canterbury. Cantuar., it
appears, had sent an address to the Queen,
commencing with, " We, the Archbishops
" and undersigned Bishops of *the Church of*
" *England.*"

" It is with much regret," said the protest, " and not without apprehension, that
" we have observed the title by which your
" Grace and the Archbishop of York, together
" with the suffragan Bishops of the two
" provinces under your jurisdiction, have
" designated yourselves in addressing our
" Sovereign, a title which, we beg permission
" to say, is unknown to the law of the land,
" and which imparts a virtual denial of the

" fifth article of union between England and
" Ireland. Your Grace is aware that, by the
" statute 39 & 40 Geo. III., c. 67, it is
" enacted ' that the Churches of England
" ' and Ireland as now by law established,
" ' be united into one Protestant Episcopal
" ' Church, to be called the United Church of
" ' England and Ireland.' "

The Archbishop of Canterbury, in reply,
acknowledged that it would have been better
to have indited the inharmonious sentence
of " the English Archbishops and Bishops of
" the United Church of England and Ireland,"
than to have given ground for the apprehen-
sions expressed.

Dr. Whately paid the penalty of prolific
authorship by obtaining the credit or discredit of not a few books to which he could
lay no claim. " The Vestiges of the Natural
" History of Creation " were, for example,
laid at his door. Nothing could be more wild
or blasphemous than the opinions advanced in
this publication, and yet good-natured people
were found to trace it on internal evidence
to the Archiepiscopal pen. Shortly after the
publication of Moore's " Travels of an Irish

" Gentleman in search of a Religion," a reply
appeared containing some acrimonious remarks of a polemical character, which Dr.
Whately—at least just then—would have
been very unlikely to write, and yet Moore
" found from Lady Elizabeth that the Arch-
" bishop of Dublin was, at first, supposed
" to have been the author of the answer."
" After all," adds Moore, " it is probably no
" Bishop at all;* but merely somebody who
" wants to be a bishop." The author was,
we believe, the late Rev. Mortimer O'Sulli-
van ; but we have also seen the work attributed to Blanco White.

Dr. Whately, as has been alleged by Dean
West, was also suspected of having been the
author of an ingenious hoax, which, pur-
porting to be a Pastoral Letter from Pope
Gregory the Sixteenth, and addressed to the
Puseyite clergy at Oxford, excited considerable attention, until a counter-pamphlet from
Dr. Pusey, analytically testing it, exposed
the trick.   The real author was Charles

* " Moore's Memoirs and Journal," edited by Lord
John Russell, vol. vii. p. 27.

Dickenson, afterwards Anglican Bishop of
Meath.

Pamphlet after pamphlet dropped from his
hand, some anonymously, and others only
partially inspired by the inexhaustible foun-
tain of his flowing thought. To one of these
a note from Dean West refers :—

"PALACE, 10*th April*, 1850.

"MY DEAR SIR,—

"The little tract you inquire about is
"entitled ' *Tractatus tres de Locis quibus-*
"' *dam difficilioribus Scripturæ Sacræ. Stut-*
"'*gartiæ*, 1849,' not directly the Arch-
"bishop's work, but was written by a person
"well read in the Archbishop's writings and
"possessing access to his unwritten views.
"And, again, the Latin rendering is by a
"different hand, and not always of the finest
"Ciceronian.

"Very sincerely yours,

"J. WEST."

CHAPTER III.

WHEN the British Association for the Advancement of Science met in Belfast in 1852, Dr. Whately, who presided over the section devoted to Statistics, took occasion to complain that the members of the press had abused their privilege by publishing a very inaccurate report of the proceedings. On their way back to Dublin, the Archbishop's travelling companion directed his attention, in the train, to a very violent retort upon him in the shape of a lengthy and rather scurrilous leader. Dr. Whately read every line attentively, and at length returned the paper, merely observing, " I intended to " sting him—I didn't think I had done it so " well."

On the occasion of this visit to Belfast, the Archbishop was entertained at dinner by

Mr. B ——, with several of the northern great guns, including Dr. Cooke and Dr. Montgomery.

The conversation turned on the subject of gaming, and the Archbishop asked any member of the company to state in what its moral offence consisted. One Reverend gentleman maintained that gaming involved no moral transgression whatever, and ought to be regarded, chiefly, as a healthful relaxation for the overtasked mind. Dr. H——, who had filled the Whately Chair of Political Economy, advanced it as his opinion that the moral offence, implied by the Archbishop, consisted in prostituting to bad purposes the talents given by God for successful · commercial speculation, in the same way as the commerce of prostitution degrades and checks marriage. "That is a very good " answer for a Political Economist," replied Dr. Whately, " but my view is simply that " inasmuch as all gaming implies a desire of " profiting at the expense of your neighbour, " it involves a breach of the tenth com- " mandment."

On another occasion he said :—

" *The best throw with the dice is, to throw* " *them away.*"

The Archbishop's points, at dinner or otherwise, were often of a more broadly humorous character, especially if he thought that his presence infused any feeling of awe or restraint. When a pause occurred, he would sometimes rouse the drooping embers, by a touch of what he called " his hot poker." On one of these occasions he called out to the host, " Mr. ——" (another pause, during which all ears were pricked up), " Mr. ——, " what is the proper female companion for " this John Dory ? " Several guesses were advanced, but none hit the right nail, until his Grace, amidst convulsions of laughter, cried, " Anne Chovy ! " A kindred " Con " of his was, " What is the female of a *mail* " coach ?" Answer—"A *mis*carriage." Having thus set the fun of the company afire, no end of jokes about Sally Lun, Dick Canter, &c. &c., followed.

Leaving to professional critics the task of sounding the depths of Whately's pellucid intellect, we shall—in the belief that in doing so we best consult the reader's fancy—proceed to gather the sparkling bubbles which played upon the surface of his sagacity.

The books of the National Board having obtained an official footing in England, from their insertion on the List of the "Committee "of Council on Education," and of the English Poor Law Commissioners, the leading London publishers, Longman, Murray, &c., addressed an argumentative remonstrance to the Lords of the Treasury, in 1853, protesting against this violation of the principles of Free Trade, by which they were first taxed, as citizens, to support the National Schools in Ireland, and next driven out of the market, as traders, the Irish Board having undertaken the general business of publishers, not alone for their own schools, but for all other schools, English as well as Irish, and applied the very taxes raised to undersell the taxpayers in their business, and obtain a monopoly of their trade. A protracted correspondence ensued between the Treasury, the publishers, and the National Board, which eventuated in the withdrawal from the Board, in 1851-2, of the privilege of supplying any save their own schools with their books. Though the Archbishop was a theoretical Free Trader, his own personal interest, as author and proprietor, lying, in this instance, on the side of monopoly, he used the keenness of his wit as well as the weight of his argument against the London publishers, and in favour of Protection. Sir Charles Wood having been said to be a warm supporter of the Free Trade.party, Dr. Whately, when the matter fell under discussion at the Board, observed, " Why, the " Treasury appear to think Wood the lignum " *vitæ* of the party, but I think a more correct " estimate of him would be lignum *inutile*."*

After the suicide of John Sadleir, whose marvellous career and monster frauds Mr. Lever has celebrated in " Davenport Dunne," a series of articles appeared in an Irish serial, labouring, with much logical acumen, to prove that John Sadleir was not dead, after all, and that he crowned his career of crime

---

* " Olim truncus eram ficulnus, inutile lignum."— Hor. Sat. VIII.

by forging his own body ! To these amusing
papers the initials of Dr. Whately were appended ; but the signature was a hoax, and
merely aimed to satirize his "Historic
" Doubts." Talking over this pleasant whim
one day, the Archbishop is said to have suddenly inquired of a party present, who was
whispered to have received some office
through the influence of Sadleir, " By the
" way, Mr. ——, why is your late friend like
" the Commander in Chief ? Simply," he
went on to say, " because he made a General
" Hall and Major Fortune " (a *general hawl*
and *made your* fortune). The allusion is to
two military gentlemen known to both, and
the former of whom was a neighbour of Dr.
Whately's near Roebuck.

" I hope your Grace will excuse my preach-
" ing next Sunday," said a parson, who was
fonder of the cushions of his easy chair than
of the cushions of his pulpit. " Certainly ! "
said the Metropolitan, indulgently. Sunday
came, and the Archbishop said to him,
" Well ! Mr. ——, what became of you—we
" expected you to preach to-day. " " Oh,
" your Grace said you would excuse my

" preaching to-day." " Exactly ; but I did
" not say I would excuse you *from* preaching."

" I was very much pleased with one passage
" in your sermon," remarked Dr. Hall to the
preacher of an interminably prolix homily.
" Which was that ? " replied the other, with
an eager smile of complacent suavity. " The
" passage from the pulpit to the vestry ! "
was the rejoinder. This anecdote is not a
bad companion to a story which Dr. Whately
told at a banquet given by the Lord-Lieutenant of Ireland about this time, and apropos
to a grace of very unusual length, which some
ecclesiastic usurped the Archbishop's place
by giving forth sonorously.

" My lord," said the Archbishop, " did
" you ever hear the story of Lord Mul-
" grave's chaplain ? " " No ! " said the
Lord-Lieutenant. " A young chaplain had
" preached a sermon of great length. ' Sir,'
" said Lord Mulgrave, bowing to him, ' there
" ' were some things in your sermon of to-
" ' day I never heard before.' ' O, my lord,'
" said the flattered chaplain, ' it is a common
" ' text, and I could not have hoped to have
" ' said anything new on the subject.' ' I

" ' *heard the clock strike twice*,' said Lord
" Mulgrave."

The conundrums also continued unflag-
gingly. On the occasion of a meeting at the
Famine Board, he asked his next neighbour
" Why Ireland was the richest country in
" the world." " Because its *capital* is always
" *Dublin* " (doubling). And in reference to
the Wicklow Railway, he asked " Why it was
" the most unmusical line in the world :"
Answer—" Because it has a Bray, a Dun-
" drum, and a Still-organ " (his own station)
" upon it." To a person who, when asked a
puzzling query, invariably closed his eyes in
the intensity of the effort to solve it, the
Archbishop said, " Sir, you resemble an
" ignorant pedagogue, who keeps his pupils
" in darkness."

" Why does the operation of hanging kill
" a man ?" inquired Dr. Whately. A physio-
logist replied, " Because inspiration is checked,
" circulation stopped, and blood suffuses and
" congests the brain." " Bosh ! " replied his
Grace, " it is because the rope is not long
" enough to let his feet touch the ground."

At the Board of the University Commission

in 1851, Dr. Whately was an active worker.
It often happens in the case of commissions,
that the commissioners, instead of concentrating their attention on the great objects
of their appointment, interfere with the
secretary's province, and fritter away their
time by writing his more important letters—
merely leaving to him the mechanical labour
of transcription — and authorizing him to
append no original matter but his signature.
To the progressive and vigilant tact of the
secretary, this commission owed much. " If
" I keep a dog," said the Archbishop,
" why should I take the bother of barking
" myself? "

But few knew better how to bark when he
liked. In the following year we find him
raising his voice lustily in the shape of a
lecture " On the Supposed Dangers of a
" little Learning." This was delivered at
Cork, in connection with the National Industrial Exhibition, of which that city had just
then been the theatre. The lecture was able
and sparkling. In introducing it, he naively
observed, that of all the instruments which
he had inspected at the exhibition that

day, none seemed so important as a good instructor. " The flax growing in the field " is not more different from the finest and " most finished cambric, than an ignorant " man is from a well-informed man." A delicate irony pervaded this lecture.

While referring to the progressive alliance of religion and physical science, for which, in opposition to the *Westminster Review*, he was anxious, he thus handled ·the sceptic's argument.

" The reviewer would speak of going ' in " ' a straightforward line ' from this place " to that, and being there before ' sunset;' " but this phrase, though common, is " scientifically untrue, like the well-known " scriptural facts of the sun standing still, " &c.; yet would the reviewer speak of " going ' in a geodesic line ' from this place to " that, and being there ' before that portion " ' of the earth was withdrawn from the " ' sun's rays ?' "

It was the Archbishop's lot to find his theories often met and thwarted by people thrusting forward their " common sense " and " experience." At such folk he took a tilt.

" In former times," he said, " men knew
" by experience that the earth stands still,
" and the sun rises and sets.   Common
" sense taught them, that there would be
" no antipodes since men could not stand
" with their heads downwards, like flies on
" the ceiling.   Experience taught the King
" of Bantam that water can never become
" solid.   And to come to the case of human
" affairs—the experience and common sense
" of the most intelligent of the Roman
" historians, Tacitus, taught him that for a
" mixed government to be established, com-
" bining the elements of royalty, aristocracy,
" and democracy, would be next to impos-
" sible ; and that if it were established, it
" must speedily be dissolved.   Yet had he
" lived to the present day, he would have
" learned that the establishment and con-
" tinuance of such a form of government
" was not impossible.   So much for expe-
" rience !   The experience of some persons
" resembles the learning of a man who has
" turned over the pages of a great many
" books without ever having learned to
" read ; and their so-called common sense

" is often in reality nothing else than com-
" mon prejudice."

The Archbishop would seem to have had
an old grudge against that troublesome
opponent " common sense." When he began
his " Logic " at Oxford, it was assumed that
a theory which does not tend to the improvement of practice is unworthy of regard, and
by the same parties it was contended that
logic has no such tendency, on the plea that
men may and do reason correctly without
it. "Many," said Whately, writing in 1826,
" many who allow the use of systematic
" principles in other things, are accustomed
" to cry up common sense as the sufficient
" and only safe guide in reasoning. Now by
" common sense is meant, I apprehend (when
" the term is used with any distinct mean-
" ing), an exercise of the judgment unaided
" by any art or system of rules; such an
" exercise as we must necessarily employ in
" numberless cases of daily occurrence; in
" which, having no established principles to
" guide us,—no line of procedure, as it were,
" distinctly chalked out,—we must needs act
" on the best extemporaneous conjectures we

" can form. He who is eminently skilful in
" doing this, is said to possess a superior
" degree of common sense. But that com-
" mon sense is only our second best guide—
" that the rules of art, if judiciously framed,
" are always desirable when they can be had,
" is an assertion, for the truth of which I
" may appeal to the testimony of mankind
" in general, which is so much the more
" valuable inasmuch as it may be accounted
" the testimony of adversaries. For the
" generality have a' strong predilection in
" favour of common sense, except in those
" points in which they respectively possess
" the knowledge of a system of rules; but
" in these points they deride any one who
" trusts to unaided common sense. A sailor,
" e. g., will, perhaps, despise the pretensions
" of medical men, and prefer treating a
" disease by common sense; but he would
" ridicule the proposal of navigating a ship
" by common sense, without regard to the
" maxims of nautical art. A physician,
" again, will perhaps contemn systems of
" Political Economy, of Logic or Metaphysics,
" and insist on the superior wisdom of

" trusting to common sense in such matters;
" but he would never approve of trusting
." to common sense in the treatment of
" disease."*

On the Cork Exhibition, an important
event in the life of Archbishop Whately
hinged. Hitherto we have glanced at his
lecture only superficially. Presently we shall
probe deep and deeper.

Meanwhile, a new "difficulty," in the
person and writings of another "Paul,"
presented itself, with which Dr. Whately
found it not so congenial to grapple, as his
" Difficulties in the Writings of Paul," published by Mr. Parker. A preamble, however,
is necessary.

On the death of Archbishop Murray, in
1852, some important changes hinged. This
respected prelate, who had passed through
times of trial and oppression, was distinguished for the conciliatory character of his
advances, and the singular moderation of his
views theological and political.

* " Elements of Logic," fourth edition, 1831,
pp. xiii, xv.

Long after the shackles had been unlocked
and the scourge had ceased to strike, the
impress of both remained upon his frame.
In 1798, this eminently inoffensive priest
had been fired at by Orange yeomen; and
he was obliged to swim across a river from
their pursuing aim. This system of persecution, sometimes on a smaller, sometimes
on a larger scale, stung Dr. Murray for
many years after. In 1798, all the Roman
Catholic chapels of Dublin were on the point
of being closed up by the despotic order of
Government; a fate averted only by the
most prompt influential and diplomatic intervention.

Although Mr. Stanley, in unfolding his
plan of the National System of Education,
arranged that approved portions of Sacred
History should be read by the children, Dr.
Whately was considered to have somewhat
departed from the spirit of the system by
introducing a volume of " Scripture Extracts
" and Lessons on the Truth of Christianity,"
which, with the sanction of the Board,
continued to be read during school hours
from 1834 until the death of Dr. Murray,

near twenty years subsequently.* The Roman Catholic Primate, Dr. Murray, was succeeded by Dr. Cullen, a prelate of considerably
more active vigilance and uncompromising
principle ; who, shortly after grasping the
helm of his diocese, detected and announced
" Breakers ahead ! " For two-and-twenty
years Dr. Whately may be said to have had
the complete direction of the youthful mind
of Ireland. Every book in their hands ema-
nated from the Palace in Stephen's Green ;

---

* In the Parliamentary proceedings of the day, the
following interesting circumstance transpires,—the suggestion of Dr. Murray's appointment is said to have
originated with Dr. Whately.

" Colonel Verner had seen, in an account of the obse-
" quies of the late Roman Catholic Archbishop of Dublin,
" as published in an Irish newspaper, a statement attri-
" buted to the Rev. gentleman who preached the sermon
" on that occasion, to the effect that at one time that
" eminent prelate had been offered the position of a privy
" councillor in the Irish Government, but had declined to
" accept it. He (Colonel Verner) had the permission of
" the noble lord, the member for London, to ask him
" whether that statement was true.

" Lord J. Russell replied, that the fact referred to by
" the hon. and gallant colonel was materially correct.
" He should not certainly have come forward unsolicited
" to make the statement, but having been asked the

the very head-pieces of the copy-books were apophthegms of Dr. Whately's composition; and, without touching on polemics, aimed at a propagandism of his views. He was the mountain from the summit of which flowed the stream that soon expanded into a vast and irresistibly rushing river, whereof daily drank ten thousand teachers and eight hundred thousand pupils. But a storm was brewing, and everybody knows that the higher the mountain the wilder the storm which beats about its head.

" question, he had no hesitation in saying that during " the period when Lord Besborough was at the head of " the Government in Ireland, it was proposed to invite " Archbishop Murray to take his seat in the Irish Privy " Council, and that the Right Rev. Prelate declined to " accept that distinction. And he could only add that " it gave him great satisfaction to make that proposal, " and it was with much regret that he found it was not " accepted by a prelate whose character he esteemed and " whose memory he revered. (Hear, hear.)"

Dr. Murray having declined the proffered honour, wrote to acquaint the Pope with his decision. The reply of his Holiness, in which he strongly eulogizes the prudence of Dr. Murray's view of the question, is still in existence. In the file of the *Morning Register* for October, 1831, there is noticed a curious report of the elevation to the Peerage of Drs. Murray and Doyle !

A detail of the exact circumstances which led to Dr. Whately's withdrawal from an institution to which he was so attached, over which he exercised such absolute sway and influence, and disconnection with which so distressed and aggrieved him, must possess peculiar interest, yet, notwithstanding that a Select Committee of the House of Lords sat for six months, in 1854, investigating the question, scores of witnesses having been examined, including the chief actors in the scene, and numbers of Parliamentary papers, pamphlets, and charges having been issued on the matter, still the history of the transaction yet remains to be written. This history we are now in a position to supply.

Following on the Great London Exhibition of 1851, came that modest but excellent Cork Exhibition, opened 10th June, 1852, to which we have already adverted. The committee determined to add to its effectiveness by a course of lectures delivered in the pavilion of the Exhibition building; and on the application of the Executive Committee, supported by Dr. Wilson, then Bishop of Cork, Dr. Whately consented to deliver the Inaugural

Lecture of the series, on Tuesday, 29th June, 1852. The subject selected by him was Popular Education, and although the lecture was delivered before a crowded, brilliant, and distinguished auditory, yet few amongst the number understood the deep design which underlay the elaborate and subtle discourse which they applauded that evening. To fully understand the lecturer's position, a slight retrospect is absolutely necessary. In August, 1850, a National Council of the Roman Catholic Hierarchy was held, in Thurles, by direction of Pope Pius IX., under the presidency of Most Rev. Dr. Cullen, R. C. Primate of All Ireland and Delegate Apostolic, and on the 23rd May, 1851, the decrees of this council were approved and confirmed by the Holy See. The Pope, by a rescript, dated October, 1847, while condemning the scheme of education in the Queen's Colleges, recommended the establishment of a Catholic University in Ireland, founded on the model of that which the prelates of Belgium had erected in the city of Louvain; and one of the chief objects in convoking the National Council in Thurles, was to give efficacy to this recommendation. Immediately after the close of the proceedings at that assembly, two lengthened addresses to the Catholics of Ireland were published, one from the Fathers of the Synod, the other from the Committee appointed by that body to enter upon the establishment of the projected Catholic University, in both of which the whole principle of education is discussed from, of course, a Catholic stand-point. In those documents* the principle is maintained that education is a *whole* which cannot, without the greatest danger, be imparted in two different divisions, secular and religious, a separation often most difficult to effect, whilst the total exclusion of the teaching of Revealed Truth, and of all positive Faith from education, is baneful in the highest degree.

Very Rev. Dr. John Henry Newman, the Archbishop's old friend and fellow student, now a Catholic Priest of the Oratory, had, by a strange coincidence, just been nominated

---

* The Papal rescripts on the Queen's Colleges and the Synodical Address of the Council of Thurles are quoted by the Hon. Baron Hughes.—*Report of Royal Commissioners on Endowed Schools*, vol. ii. p. 380.

Rector of the Catholic University of Ireland. Dr. Whately and Dr. Newman—the former as the great champion of the National System and of its further development in the Queen's Colleges, the latter as the embodiment of the antagonistic principle that the Church has obtained a Divine mission to teach faith and morals, and to supervise even all secular teaching, so far as it may peril or affect these—after a college separation of many years, suddenly find themselves arrayed against each other, athletes in the arena of one of the greatest controversies of modern times in Ireland.

Amongst all the Oxford men with whom Whately had associated, there were few between whom closer relations or a more intimate friendship existed than Dr. Whately and Dr. Newman.*

---

* A correspondent sends us the following note :—

" The quarter of a century that Dr. Whately spent
" in Oxford brought him into intimate relations with a
" galaxy of men that in their respective careers attained
" the highest eminence in the councils of the State, in
" the Church, at the Bar, in the Senate, in science and
" in literature. Sir Robert Peel, the Earl of Derby,

We may further preface coming remarks by observing that the project of District Model Schools, four of which had been opened in 1849, the same year that the Queen's Colleges were brought into operation, had just received unexpected opposition, an opposition that has since been steadily extending. The National Board, desirous to establish a Model School in Drogheda, a project which had received very influential local support, were opposed and defeated by the influence of Archbishop Cullen, appointed to the see of Armagh, February 1850, whose letter to Alderman Boyglan, denouncing the project, aroused the hostility of the Corporation and of all the Catholics of the borough

" the Earl of Carlisle, Gladstone, Cardwell, Labouchere,
" Bethell (present Lord Chancellor of England), Wood
" (Sir Charles), Copleston (Bishop of Llandaff), Thirlwall
" (St. David's), Hinds (Norwich), Phillpotts (Exeter),
" Tait (London), Longley (Archbishop of Canterbury),
" Wilberforce (Oxford), Milman, Arnold, Pusey,
" Newman, Keble, Oakeley, Wilberforce (W. and
" Henry W.) Faber, the Earl of Rosse, Daubeny, Froude,
" Nassau Senior, and a host of men only a little less
" distinguished, were contemporaries of Dr. Whately in
" Oxford."

against it.   This opposition, through the
example and influence of Dr. Cullen, spread
to Waterford in 1851, when the Bishop,
nearly all the Catholic clergy, and most of
the laity, opposed the project for erecting a
Model School in that city.   The lamented
death of Archbishop Murray, from the first a
member of the National Board, early in 1852,
and the translation of Dr. Cullen, the avowed
opponent of that system, to the see of
Dublin, in May, showed Dr. Whately that
the opposition to the Government scheme of
education, primary and collegiate, was assum-
ing a very formidable aspect.   All these
circumstances tended to inspire Dr. Whately
to concentrate his genius and ability in
one great effort to expose, if possible, the
weakness of the principles put forth by the
Catholic party, and thereby to avert the
threatened overthrow of a system largely
sustained by his continuous advocacy and
support.   On this point more will be found
in our next chapter.

CHAPTER IV.

Dr. WHATELY divided his inaugural lecture
at the Cork Exhibition into two heads; one,
a defence of what is called *Popular* Education,
against the argument which Pope is alleged
to have set forth in the well-known line—

"A little learning is a dangerous thing;"

the other, the dangers to be apprehended
from the educational principle laid down by
Catholics, that their Church, through her
ministers, should exercise supervision or
control over secular education. The opening
of the lecture, in which Dr. Whately vin-
dicates the superiority of the educator over
every other object in the Industrial Exhibition, is extremely characteristic :—

"The proposed lectures should be con-
"sidered as emanating from—as the off-

" spring of—the National Exhibition ; and, in
" fact, may be considered as a subsidiary
" and necessary portion of it. These lectures
" do not undertake or pretend to give a
" course of education in any one particular
" department, any more than the collection
" of manufactures and articles, viewed this
" day, should be considered as a warehouse,
" rather than a sample of what nature and
" art were capable of producing in this
" country. Such an exhibition, I take it,
" would be unfinished and incomplete unless
" some specimens were also exhibited of
" what could be done, *in the way of instruction,*
" by those whom the country could produce
" to give that instruction to the nation. Of
" all the instruments which are exhibited in
" the collection that I have inspected in the
" course of this day, *there is none so important*
" *as a good instructor.*"

The main object of his Grace's discourse,
a reply to the arguments advanced in the
several recent addresses of the Catholic
hierarchy to their flocks, in the matter of
schemes of education, is thus adroitly set
forth :—

" But we will be told by some, that ' they
" ' wish only secular education to be under
" ' the control of those who have the
" ' spiritual guidance of the persons receiving
" ' such secular education ; ' that ' those
" ' spiritual directors should have a vote
" ' upon everything which has reference to
" ' the secular education, because,' they
" add, ' the lecturer on geology might, in the
" ' course of his address, insinuate false and
" ' mischievous notions in regard to religion
" ' and morality; and, therefore, the entire
" ' control of the secular education should
" ' be placed under the guidance and super-
" ' intendence of the spiritual guides of the
" ' people.' Now, as to the danger in
" question, I will not deny that it is *possible*
" for a teacher of some branch of secular
" learning to introduce false religious notions,
" and mischievous and dangerous moral prin-
" ciples. But I do not think there is any
" adequate safeguard against such danger,
" except to warn men against it, and to tell
" them to teach merely geology, mathematics,
" agriculture, &c., in their respective depart-
" ments ; but, in so doing, to take care that

" they do not insinuate anything against
" religious and moral principles.　For if you
" go beyond this precaution, there is a
" danger on the opposite side.　If you leave
" the teaching of geology and mathematics
" to the *spiritual* teachers of the people,
" you may find that these may make as
" great errors as the others, by teaching
" false philosophical principles. ' What, a
" ' different kind of danger ? ' it may be said.
" ' Suppose a man did imbibe some false
" ' notions of philosophy—how trifling is this
" ' in comparison with his imbibing false re-
" ' ligious and dangerous moral principles ! '
" ' May not a man,' they continue, ' be a
" ' good Christian, although a bad chemist ?
" ' May not a man be a good Christian,
" ' although he believes the sun goes round
" ' the earth ? '　Now this I hold to be
" an erroneous view of the case.　You will
" perceive, on reflection, *the danger is nearly*
" *the same, and not less, but greater.*　False
" philosophical notions, unduly conveyed by
" professors who are the spiritual teachers
" of the people, if given merely as their own
" private opinions as individuals, and not

" as interwoven with their religious teaching,
" are no greater evil than if taught by any
" one else. But it is not so with errors in
" science, when represented as connected
" with religion. Although errors in chemistry
" and physics are, in themselves, com-
" temptible when compared with the danger
" of wrong notions in religion and morality,
" there is danger of persons being taught
" certain erroneous notions of philosophy
" *as a part of their religion*, and, by that
" means, having a lever placed under their
" religious principles, which will upheave
" and overturn them. True, a man may be a
" good Christian and a moral man, though he
" believe the sun moves round the earth ; but
" suppose that a man was taught, as a part
" of *divine revelation*, and an essential point
" of his faith, that the sun really does move
" round the earth, then, when it is demon-
" strated to him that such is not the fact,
" he is thus led to believe that he has got
" a system of wrong notions *as his religious*
" *faith*, and he will be inclined to doubt
" it all."

The report of the lecture, published by the

executive committee, with the caution that
they are not responsible for the opinions
contained in it, adds, that "much valuable
" matter was omitted by the reporters, and
" his Grace's more pressing avocations have
" prevented him from supplying the omis-
" sions." A member of the audience, one
especially interested in the subject, enables
us to complete an important portion of this
branch of the lecture.   Dr. Whately, in
continuation, went on to show that the
Catholic system was a striking example of
the fallacy of Thaumatrope.   Thus, in youth,
spirituals and seculars become so united, as
to direction, in the mind's eye, that, constantly whirled, infallible in one is transferred
to infallible in the other; whereas, in manhood, the same fallacy will correct and overthrow the system; thus false philosophy
proved in seculars is extended to spirituals,
authority in which becomes thereby over-
thrown, to the utter destruction of all Church
authority in the matter of education.*

* " It will often happen that when two objects are
" *incompatible*, though either of them, *separately*, may

His Grace was warmly applauded by the crowded and distinguished audience repeatedly during, and with marked emphasis at the close of, this brilliant lecture.

" be attained, the incompatibility is disguised by a rapid
" and frequent transition from the one to the other
" alternately. Two distinct objects may, by being
" dexterously presented, again and again, in quick suc-
" cession, to the mind of a cursory reader, be so
" associated together, *in his thoughts*, as to be conceived
" capable, when in fact they are not, of being *actually*
" combined in practice. The fallacious belief, thus
" induced, bears a striking resemblance to the optical
" illusion effected by that ingenious and philosophical
" toy called the *thaumatrope ;* in which two objects,
" painted on opposite sides of a card,—for instance a
" man and a horse—a bird and a cage,—are, by a quick
" rotatory motion, made to impress the eye, in combina-
" tion, so as to form one picture of the man on the
" horse's back, the bird in the cage, &c. As soon as
" the card is allowed to remain at rest the figures, of
" course, appear as they really are, separate, and on
" opposite sides. A mental illusion, closely analogous
" to this, is produced, when by a rapid and repeated
" transition from one subject to another, alternately, the
" mind is deluded into an idea of the actual combi-
" nation of things that are really incompatible. A very
" moderate degree of calm and fixed attention soon
" shows that the two objects are painted on opposite
" sides of the card."—Whately's *Logic*, book iii. § 11.

While coffee was being served, after the lecture, a seemingly unimportant incident occurred, which subsequently led to grave influences in reference both to the lecturer and to his subject. Mr. Kavanagh, now Professor in the Catholic University, was then, and from the year 1847 had been, Head Inspector of National Schools in the Munster Circuit, of which Cork was the centre.

He had just arrived in Cork, from Dunmanway, a small town to the west of Bandon, the day before the lecture, to select the books to be given as premiums at the public examination about to be held in the Model School of Dunmanway, and; seeing the lecture advertised, he attended it, and during coffee, presented himself to the Archbishop, and invited his Grace, if he was making any stay in Cork, to go to Dunmanway to attend the public examination of the Model Schools. Dr. Whately replied, that he would be very happy to attend, were he able, but that he was leaving Cork next morning for Clonmel, where he was going on a visit to Lady Osborne, at Newtownanner. Mr. Kavanagh then reminded his Grace that when he was last in Clonmel, he visited the Model School there, but it was vacation time, and now that the schools were in operation, he hoped the Archbishop would call there during his visits to Newtownanner. His Grace said that it would give him great pleasure to do so, asked Mr. Kavanagh could he go to Clonmel, the better to enable his Grace to examine the Model Schools, a request at once acceded to by the head inspector, who postponed his other official engagements to wait on the Archbishop. Next morning, 30th June, Dr. Whately and Mr. Kavanagh went from Cork to Clonmel, the Archbishop proceeding to Newtownanner, where his son-in-law was staying on a visit, and by arrangement, the head inspector met his Grace, accompanied by Lady Osborne, Mrs. Bernal Osborne, and Mr. Wale, Dr. Whately's son-in-law, next morning, 1st July, at 11 o'clock, at the Model School, Clonmel. The project of District Model Schools, though early formed, was not brought into operation until 1849, the same year that the Queen's Colleges were opened. In the summer of that year, four of them sprung into operation, one in Newry, another in Ballymena, a third in Dunmanway, and the fourth in Clonmel, and from the novelty of the scheme, the very respectable programme of education which they presented, the elegance of the fabrics, the low, almost nominal, rates of fees, and the general attractiveness of the establishments, they excited a large and very marked share of public attention. The Clonmel Model School was placed under the direction of Mr. Kavanagh, head inspector, whose practical skill and experience as an educationist were effectively brought to bear in working every branch of the establishment; and this, combined with his popularity with the Catholic clergy and people, soon placed the Clonmel Model Schools at the head of all these new enterprises. Children of the highest social rank and of every creed in the town attended the schools, distinguished visitors, English and Irish, were attracted to it by the excellence of its reputation; and anxious to procure similar advantages for their own children, the citizens of Limerick, Waterford, Kilkenny, and other

important towns, applied to the National
Board to establish Model Schools in those
places. Under all these circumstances, it
was a natural, official, and professional display, on the part of the head inspector, to
show his Grace, Dr. Whately, the chairman
of the board, the fruits of his administrative
ability, and the Archbishop, on his part,
appeared no less anxious to fully test the
claims of the schools to the very high reputation which they had acquired. His Grace
spent four hours in the establishment, sometimes examining the classes himself, and
sometimes hearing the inspector, the head
inspector, or the teachers, examine on subjects selected by him; and the minuteness of
his inquiries may be understood from the
following amongst many of the incidents that
occurred during the examination. While in
the Infants' School, the mistress got some
of the youngest of the children to recite little
pieces of poetry. When the exercise was
over, his Grace, turning to the head inspector, said, " Mr. Kavanagh, take care,
" do these children *understand* what they
" have recited?" " Likely some of them do

" not," said the · inspector, " but I can
" assure your Grace that even here, the
" teaching is *thorough*, and any little ones
" that do not understand the verses will
" soon be taught their meaning." " Oh,
" Mr. Kavanagh," said his Grace, " surely
" you do not advocate that they should
" swallow their food first and chew it after-
" wards."*   " Well, my Lord," was the

---

* He varied this idea on another occasion thus :—

" The knowledge of facts, whether much or little,
" will often be worse than useless to those who are
" deficient in the power of discriminating and selecting,
" just as food is to a body, whose digestive system is so
" much impaired as to be incapable of separating the
" nutritious portions."

These and other retorts which at the time of their
utterance were regarded as singularly felicitous, only
furnish fresh confirmation of the aphoristic platitude,
" There is nothing new under the sun."   Take up
the seventh volume of " Moore's Diary" (p. 60), and
we find :—

" Rogers in speaking of Brougham and remarking
" how well he often puts some points in his speeches,
" gave as an instance what he had said in a late speech
" on the subject of very young men at college signing
" the Thirty-nine Articles ; viz. :   that they swallowed
" them first and digested them afterwards.   On hearing

reply, " in practice it is found necessary
" to treat such little children occasionally as
" *ruminants*, the process of mental assimila-
" tion not being complete until they have
" chewed their food even several times after
" they have swallowed it." " It may be,"
said the Archbishop, enjoying how his own
illustration had been promptly turned against
him; " but when Mrs. Whately and I got

" this, I could not help quietly putting in a claim for
" my own property, which the thought in question
" decidedly was; as not more than a week before
" Brougham made this speech my verses on Phillpotts'
" famous explanation of the signing had appeared in the
" *Times*, and that Brougham must have read those verses,
" his immediate interest in the subject was a sufficient
" guarantee. In that squib were the following lines :—

" ' Both in dining and signing we take the same plan,
" ' First swallow all down, then digest—as we can.' "

" When I mentioned this, Rogers seemed a little
" ashamed of himself. It is too hard when a great gun
" like the Chancellor condescends to discharge one of
" my pellets from his muzzle, that the original *pop-gun*
" should be thus forgotten. But so it is : station makes
" all the difference, even in a joke, and Shakespeare was
" for once wrong when he said, ' a jest's prosperity lies
" ' not in the tongue of him who makes it,' for it does
" sometimes lie wholly there."

" married, one of the first things that we
" agreed upon was that, should Providence
" send us children, we would never teach them
" anything that they did not understand."
" Not even their prayers, my Lord?" replied Mr. Kavanagh.   " Yes, not even their
" prayers," said the Archbishop.   " What
" then becomes," retorted the head inspector,
" of the Apostle's injunction to hold a sound
" form of words?"   An earnest discussion
of the true principles of teaching followed
between the Archbishop and the head inspector, in the course of which his Grace
said, "I do not think, however, that you
" Roman Catholics are *entirely* open to the
" charge brought against you, that at your
" public worship you are mere *spectators*,
" the bulk of the people not understanding
" the language of your liturgy.   Presby-
" terians are only *auditors*, it is, with perhaps
" more justice, said, having no ritual or
" prayer-book, listening merely to prayers
" improvised at the moment by their minister;
" whilst Church Protestants alone are *peti-*
" *tioners*, clergy and laity having arranged
" beforehand precisely what they are about

" to ask, and the terms, in the vernacular,
" in which to supplicate for it."

"My Lord," replied Mr. Kavanagh,
" apart from all other argument that this
" charge does not justly lie against Catholics,
" the very size and shape of our superior
" churches show that neither hearing the
" priest, nor understanding the words of the
" Liturgy, is essentially necessary to con-
" stitute true and full participation in our
" worship, or to render us not mere specta-
" tors, nor auditors, like the Presbyterians,
" but rational petitioners and worshippers.
" The least instructed amongst us under-
" stands what the Mass is, and all that is
" required is to believe in its efficacy, and
" know and devoutly unite for its object, in
" order to render every one that *assists* at
" Mass a true worshipper, and to constitute
" him a petitioner for the ends of its institu-
" tion, just as every one in the city that saw
" the smoke of the victim ascending from
" the Temple of Jerusalem, by a union of
" sentiment with the worshippers participated
" in the act of adoration, whereas non-
" Catholics, who reject the commemorative

" sacrifice of the New Law are in no such
" position."

Dr. Whately liked a man to declare boldly
the faith that is in him; and the conversation
sped with pleasant animation.   But a cloud
was gathering; and, ere long, a tempest.
The Archbishop asked Mr. Kavanagh what
books they had been in the habit of reading.
" We use all the books sanctioned by the
" Board, with the exception of your Grace's,"
replied the inspector stoutly.   The Archbishop seemed unprepared for the reply, and
his lip quivered.   Was this the end of his
labours and hopes?

" How is this?" he asked, as soon as the
almost paralyzing effects of his astonishment
had tolerably subsided.   It appeared that
some of the parents of the Catholic children
had objected to the books, and in accordance
with one of the fundamental rules of the
Board, which had for some time lain a dead
letter, the use of the books was relinquished.
" And pray on what grounds are the Pro-
" testant children deprived of the books?"
continued Dr. Whately.   " You act like the
" dog in the manger.   You will neither use

" them yourselves, nor allow the Protestants
" to use them." "The Protestants were
" offered your Grace's books," said the head
inspector, "but they replied that they did
" not require them."*

Dr. Whately made no further reply, but
called for the Visitors' Book, in which he
wrote, under date, July 1st, 1852, the following remarks :—

" I find that all the books published by the
" Board are not used, the Scripture Extracts
" and the *Lessons on the Truth of Christianity*

---

* Another publication connected with these little
works, entitled "Introductory Lessons on the History of
" Religious Worship," being *a sequel* to the " Lessons on
" Christian Evidences," also published by Parker, omits
all open profession of belief in the Trinity of the Divine
Persons and Divinity of Christ ; declares that no real
priesthood exists ; and compares the Invocation of Saints
to the pagan practice of worshipping deceased men.

The first edition, published for the use of the National
Schools, and free from the graver errors just indicated,
was alleged by Dr. Whately to have been examined and
approved in Rome. In this statement there was a misapprehension. The book was examined at Dr. Murray's
instance, and neither approved nor condemned, because an
understanding took place that no one should be compelled
to use it in the schools. Since Dr. Murray's death it has
been placed on the Index Expurgatorius.

" being excluded. It appears to me most
" important that in all the schools of which
" we are patrons,—viz., the model schools,
" all our books should be read. The in-
" ference naturally to be drawn from this
" not being done is either that we are insin-
" cere in recommending books which we
" prove by our conduct we do not think well
" of, or else that we suffer this or that person
" to usurp our power and dictate to us. I
" have no doubt we shall hear of this, and
" very unpleasantly. We never compel any
" patron to use a book he does not like, or
" to abstain from the use of any sanctioned
" by us which he does not like, and we
" should exercise the same right where we
" are patrons."

The Archbishop was so excited on the
subject of his discovery, that he threw up a
local engagement which he had formed, and
hurried off by an early train to Dublin.

From the altar of every Roman Catholic
church in the dioceses of Dublin, Kildare,
Ossory, and Ferns, a Pastoral, signed by Dr.
Cullen and his three suffragans, was shortly
after read :—

" There are two little works," it went on
to say, " which have been sometimes, though
" rarely, used by Catholic children, which
" we now ask to be banished from their
" hands. The first is a little treatise on the
" evidences of Christianity, composed by a
" Protestant dignitary who has lately dis-
" tinguished himself by an unprovoked attack
" on our conventual institutions, under the
" pretence of·protecting personal liberty."

The " Lessons on the Truth of Chris-
" tianity " had been condemned quite as much
by Protestants as Catholics. It made no mention of the Divinity of our Lord ; and another
edition of it, published by Parker, of London,
in 1849, introduced a chapter not in the
Dublin edition, headed Faith and Credulity,
which was said to insinuate the Pelagian
poison — a heresy unanimously condemned
not only by Catholic but by Protestant divines.
The same chapter defined Christian faith to
be a " fairness in listening to evidence, and
" judging accordingly, without being led
" away by prejudice and inclination" (p. 22)
—a definition which, although not opposed to the teaching of most Anglican

divines, is wholly in antagonism to the doctrine of Roman Catholic theologians, who have always held with St. Paul, that faith is a gift of Heaven, which can come only from God. In the Preface it was stated :—" Another edition of this tract, " somewhat altered, has been published by " the National Education Board, under the " title of ' Lessons on the Truth of Chris- " ' tianity.' The two tracts differ in a few " places as to the arrangements of the argu- " ments and the form of expression, but not " in anything essential. Some persons prefer " the one edition, and some the other. The " Board permits the use of either of them in " the National Schools, according to the " choice of the managers. Neither of them " contains any matter of controversy among " Christians."

The " Scripture Lessons " having been searchingly analyzed by Dr. Cullen, he went on to say :—

" This little work appears to have been " compiled for the purpose of giving a united " religious instruction to Catholic and non- " Catholic children in the same class. We

" reprobate such a project. Separate reli-
" gious instruction, as it was laid down by
" a statesman who first introduced the
" national system into Ireland, is the only
" protection for Catholics. It is contrary to
" the spirit and nature of our holy Church
" to sanction united religious instruction, or
" to sanction any instruction on matters
" connected with religion given by persons
" who themselves reject the teaching of the
" Catholic Church."

The difficulty of maintaining a comfortable
position between two stools was illustrated
even in the case of these " Scripture Les-
" sons." The late Dr. Elrington, Bishop of
Ferns, and his son, the Rev. C. Elrington,
Regius Professor of Divinity in Trinity College, Dublin, raised a considerable conflag-
ration, so far back as the year 1836, by the
startling statement, that the " *adoration* of the
" Virgin Mary" was inculcated in a marginal
note by Dr. Whately to the " Scripture Ex-
" tracts." The allegation was, with others,
brought before a committee of Parliament in
1837, for investigation ; and Dr. Whately, who
denied the impeachment, was examined at

much length upon it.—*Report*, 4827-4834, &c.
The Archbishop, during the same examination, referred to a statement mentioned at
public meetings, and printed in newspaper
articles again and again, relative to a translation in the "Second Book of Extracts," in
the Gospel of St. Luke. " It was confidently
" stated," he added, " that in consequence
" of disputes at the Board, whether the word
" should be translated 'Penance' or 'Re-
" 'pentance,' it had been entirely thrown out,
" and no mention made of either. That was
" circulated while the book was in its pro-
" gress through the press. There never was
" any ground for it." The Rev. Dr. Boyton
was examined on the same occasion, and he
essayed to show the tendency of the Scripture Extracts to support the dogmas of the
Roman Catholic Church.—*Report*, 7593.

The ban pronounced by Dr. Cullen elec-
trically shot into every cabin in Leinster.
On the Monday morning following, every
Roman Catholic child, on being presented
with the " Scripture Lessons " and " Evi-
" dences of Christianity," rejected the use of
them.

The other Roman Catholic Bishops of Ireland, with one or two exceptions, echoed Dr. Cullen's judgment, and with the same results.

Fifteen Commissioners constituted the Board. Dr. Whately was absent, at that juncture, on his visitation. Lord Bellew, a Catholic peer, who had very rarely attended, was, as usual, absent. Mr. Baron Greene did not attend. The Ex-Chancellor Blackburne, Mr. Andrews, Dr. Henry, and Mr. Gibson voted against the expulsion of the " Lessons." The Right Hon. Alexander Macdonnel, the Resident Commissioner, took an opposite view, in which he was joined by two other Protestant Commissioners,—Lord Chancellor Brady and the Marquis of Kildare. Five Catholics made up, with the last-named three, the majority by which the books were ejected.

The *Times** was of opinion that the decision of the Board was sound, that Dr. Whately had not the best of the argument, and that " Dr. Cullen faithfully interpreted the prin-

* *Times*, No. 24,686.

" ciples of the Roman Catholic Church in
" this matter; as Protestants and Roman
" Catholics base the evidences of Christianity
" upon totally different grounds, they could
" not well be taught them in common, and
" there were many who concur with Mr.
" Macdonnel, the Resident Commissioner,
" that it is not expedient to put books on
" the evidences of Christianity in the hands
" of children at school between the ages of
" eight and fifteen, making them familiar
" with infidel objections, and raising doubts
" in their minds which they might never
" otherwise entertain, and which the plainest
" and most forcible reasoning might in some
" cases fail to remove."

Pending the event to which we have referred, Dr. Whately addressed the following
characteristic letter to the Lord-Lieutenant
of Ireland :—

[*Private.*]

" *5th July*, 1853.

" My dear Lord,—

" I have heard from Baron Greene, that
" (as your Excellency is doubtless aware)
" he means to move next Friday, that the

" Board should make and announce a formal
" decision on the points at issue.

" There seems good reason for his objec-
" tion to leaving matters in their present
" state, an anomalous state, which is unsatis-
" factory to *all* parties ; since each must be
" dissatisfied that their own views are not
" *fully* and generally carried out.

" I have to acknowledge also your Excel-
" lency's communication (which I should
" have replied to immediately, but for the
" pressure of business) in which you suggest
" to me to reconsider the determination I
" had formed.

" I thought I had sufficiently explained
" how fully and with what anxious care I
" *have* for *many months* considered and re-
" considered the subject ; but perhaps I may
" have failed to express myself with sufficient
" clearness, or it may be that I have con-
" fused together in my memory what I have
" said to *your Excellency* and to the late *Lord*
" *Lieutenant.*

" I may add that I have also fully and fre-
" quently discussed the subject with my most
" confidential advisers, to one of whom, the

" Bishop of Norwich, I took the liberty of
" referring Lord Aberdeen, as a person
" thoroughly acquainted with Ireland and
" with the national system, and with my
" sentiments, and who could give any need-
" ful explanations orally, much better than
" I could by letter.

" Having the advantage of possessing
" intimate friends of eminent good sense and
" worth, I felt bound to consult them, and
" listen with deference to what they might
" say. I will not say, however, that I was
" prepared, in case of finding their views
" different from my own, to alter my course
" unless they offered me stronger reasons
" than any I have ever heard. But I found
" them all fully agreed with me in thinking
" that no course is open to me consistently
" with honour but the one I have resolved
" on, and that a departure from it would be
" no less unwise than unjustifiable.

" As for my personal motives, such as
" regard for my own ease or my own credit,
" no one can think me capable of being
" influenced in the present case by any
" such considerations, who knows but the

" half of the toil I have endured and the
" obloquy and vexatious opposition I have
" encountered in the cause for above twenty-
" one years.

" And on any minor question I have always
" been ready to sacrifice my own views of
" expediency to the judgment of the other
" Commissioners. But I regard the present
" as a question not merely of expediency, but
" of principle also. I consider it was not
" only one of *vital importance to the public*,
" but also as one on which *good faith* is at
" stake. And doubtless your Excellency
" would be as far from wishing, as from ex-
" pecting, that I should take any course at
" variance with my conscientious conviction
" of duty.

" What leads some persons to take a dif-
" ferent view from mine seems to be their
" confounding together two totally different
" questions; that concerning the original
" *adoption* of some rule or some books, and
" concerning its *removal* afterwards. And
" yet no one would say that freedom to *make*,
" or refuse to make a compact, implies free-
" dom to *break* it; that because a State is

" allowed to ratify or not a certain treaty,
" therefore it is allowed to violate a treaty, or
" to modify its conditions at pleasure; that
" because a man might lawfully have remained
" single, therefore he may obtain a divorce
" whenever he thinks fit.

" Whenever any rule, or any book, was
" proposed, if any one Commissioner objected
" to the whole, or to a portion of it, I always
" at once acquiesced in its withdrawal, and in
" fact several parts of some of the books now
" in use were originally thus altered to meet
" the objection of a single Commissioner.
" If, accordingly, when some of the books
" now so much discussed were first proposed,
" any Commissioner had said, 'Although
" ' Archbishop Murray and all the other
" ' Commissioners have carefully examined
" ' this book and pronounced it sound in
" ' doctrine and suitable for united education,
" ' yet *I* think otherwise,' he would have been
" yielded to without even any remonstrance.

" But when some books or some rules
" have been deliberately sanctioned by the
" unanimous voice of the Commissioners,
" and have been for many years *appealed*

" to in vindication of the system, or as a
" *ground* on which *co-operation was invited*
" *and obtained;* if afterwards this decision
" is reversed, and this sanction withdrawn,
" such a gross breach of faith could not fail
" to deprive for ever the Commissioners, and
" all other public men who may be parties to
" it, of all public confidence, and of all just
" claims to it.

  " It would be vain to say, ' *We* think this
" ' or that a matter of very small conse-
" ' quence.' The answer would .be, (1) It·
" is *plain you did not reckon it* so when you
" brought it forward before the public as a
" strong recommendation of the · system.
" (2) *Who* is to be the judge of the compara-
" tive importance of a certain innovation ?
" *You ?* the very party introducing it ?
" Why, *every* first encroachment is either in
" itself small, or is so represented by its
" authors. And, (3) Why should we expect
" that the first step will be also the *last?*
" When once you have departed from an
" implied pledge to the public, what security
" is there that you will not introduce fresh
" and fresh violations of it ? It is to be ex-

" pected that you will go on following all the
" changes, and conforming to all the varia-
" tions of a Church which boasts of being
" unchangeable and united, but whose highest
" dignitaries pronounce that heterodox now,
" which was, in the judgment of others
" equally high, quite orthodox some years
" ago.

" When, however, I speak of the ruinous
" effect on public confidence which I am con-
" vinced would result from the proposed
" innovations, I wish it to be distinctly un-
" derstood that, even if I thought quite
" otherwise on that point, and saw a present
" worldly expediency in them, I should still
" feel *not at liberty morally* to be a party to
" them; I should feel this to be an abandon-
" ment of principle.

" But as it is, I am convinced that nothing
" would be gained—very much the reverse—
" by my continuing Commissioner under such
" an abandonment of the system hitherto pur-
" sued. I approve the system as much as
" ever, and am as ready as ever to carry it
" on, but I feel that I should be deserting
" it in the most disingenuous and the most

" mischievous way possible, were I to *pre-*
" *tend* to be carrying it on, when in reality
" subverting it. I should make the proceed-
" ings of the Board even *more* open to sus-
" picion (if possible) than they would be
" without; for if a man is liable (as he must
" be) to incur distrust and contempt for
" making unwarrantable concessions, under
" a mistaken belief that he is *acting rightly,*
" how much more, when it is *known* that his
" conviction is the very reverse?

" All the influence I have possessed has
" been based on the general belief (partaken
" of even by those most opposed to me in
" practice) of my firm and conscientious
" adherence to what I deliberately judge to
" be my duty; if I were to come forward
" acting *against* that judgment, and which
" moreover is *known* to be my judgment (for
" the late proceedings are no secret), I
" should forfeit all public confidence, and my
" support of any measure would be thence-
" forward utterly worthless.

" I have endeavoured, at the risk of being
" tedious, to lay before your Excellency as
" plainly as possible the grounds of my con-

" victions ; and whether these shall appear
" to you sufficient grounds or not, at least
" you will perceive that *with* those convic-
" tions, I cannot possibly swerve from the
" course I have resolved on.

" Believe me, &c.,

" (Signed)   Rd. Dublin.

" P.S.—I have in my possession, and can
" communicate to your Excellency if thought
" desirable, a copy of the ' Decrees of the
" ' Synod of Thurles,' relative to the national
" schools; which plainly prove (what to *me*
" had been no secret long since) their deter-
" mination not to stop short of a *complete*
" subversion of the existing system.

" If there be any one who is inclined to
" make a concession against his better judg-
" ment, in the vain hope of conciliating the
" party who demands it, and who resolves to
" concede nothing *more*, this document may
" open his eyes. He may learn from it,
" without waiting for the bitter proof of
" experience, that such a course would
" merely place him in a false position, in
" which he could neither go on nor draw
" back without disgrace."

It cannot be said that Dr. Whately's attitude on this question was inconsistent, although it may be open to other objections. In dealing as an Education Commissioner with the antagonism of Protestants, he had always consistently maintained the principle of " No Surrender." In his evidence, delivered so far back as the year 1837, he mentions that had he withdrawn the Note objected to by Bishop Elrington, in reference to the Blessed Virgin Mary, " it would " have increased instead of allayed the " hostility " [of Protestants].*

* Report, 4908.

CHAPTER V.

DR. WHATELY, finding the great labour of his episcopate foiled, lost temper, charged the National Board with breach of faith, and wrote to the Lord Lieutenant to say that if he did not receive satisfaction he would consider himself " *dismissed.*" The " My dear " Lord " had now given place to a more costive mode of epistolary salutation :—

"PALACE, *July 26th,* 1853.

" MAY IT PLEASE YOUR EXCELLENCY,—

" Pursuant to the communication made a " short time ago, I have now to announce " to Government, through your Excellency, " and to the Commissioners, that I am no " longer a member of the Education Board.

" When I found myself under the painful " necessity of appealing to your Excellency

" against the recent proceedings of the Board,
" which I regard as a departure from the
" existing system such as we were not justi-
" fied in making, I added that, if I obtained
" no redress from Government, I should con-
" sider myself as dismissed.

" I have purposely avoided using the word
" 'resignation,' lest I should be understood
" to have altered my views of the National
" System, or to withdraw from it as no longer
" approving it. The reverse is the fact. I
" am as much attached to the system as ever,
" and as ready as ever to carry it on. And
" it is precisely because I do retain these
" views that I am driven to the present step.
" Feeling that the system which has flourished
" for above twenty-one years is virtually aban-
" doned, and consequently that the office I
" have hitherto held is in reality suppressed,
" it would not be fair for me to deceive Par-
" liament and the public by pretending to
" go on, carrying out the system, which, in
" truth, is fundamentally changed.

" If I were to wait for the final determi-
" nation of Government on the matters in
" debate, the decision of the Board in the

" mean time taking effect, I should be placed
" altogether in a false position. By withholding
" my decision to withdraw, while the Com-
" missioners do not withhold theirs but carry
" it out in practice, I should be held respon-
" sible, and justly, for proceedings which I
" not only believe, but am known to believe,
" to be unjustifiable.

" When I spoke of the Commissioners
" having exceeded their ' powers,' and of
" their having no ' right' to prohibit books
" that have received the unanimous sanction
" of the Board, of course I was speaking of
" fair and equitable rights.

" As for legal rights, or obligations en-
" forced by legal penalties, these were not in
" my mind. I am considering what a man
" of honour would hold himself bound to do,
" or debarred from doing, in the faithful dis-
" charge of a public trust solemnly confided
" to him. I am well aware that a man may
" sometimes find himself so circumstanced
" as to have the ' power' with legal impu-
" nity to break faith with his neighbour, to
" disappoint reasonable expectations which
" he knows to exist, and has himself contri-

" buted to raise; to 'keep the word of
" 'promise to the ear, and break it to the
" 'hope.'

" But to any one judging fairly, it must
" be evident that the ' full control over the
" 'books to be used' given to the Commis-
" sioners, was always understood to mean
" that no books were to be used without
" their unanimous sanction, and that any
" book thus sanctioned was to be supplied
" to any school in connection with the Board,
" and might be used therein if the patron
" approved it.

" That a book so sanctioned should be
" liable to be afterwards prohibited never was
" at all contemplated by any of the Ministries
" which have supported the system, or by
" any Parliament that has voted grants to
" it, or by any Member of Parliament favour-
" able or hostile to the schools.   Never did
" any opponent come forward to say, This is
" all a delusion; we are wasting time in
" discussing the merits of these books, since
" some of them may probably be struck off
" the list next week, and some more the
" week after.   The list of books is merely a

" bait to allure the over-trustful into placing
" schools under the Board, and as soon as
" the deception has succeeded, the books
" which had chiefly aided in it will be pro-
" hibited.

" And if any one had brought forward such
" a surmise, it cannot be doubted that it
" would have been repelled with indignation
" and disgust. This being the case, it is
" plain that to depart from the system in
" this point, and to introduce an innovation
" never contemplated by any one when the
" grants were moved for and voted, would
" be to divert the public money from the
" purpose for which it was granted. And it
" is also a gross injustice towards the many
" hundred patrons of schools who were in-
" vited and induced to place them under the
" Board on the strength of an implied pro-
" mise fully understood by all parties and
" acted on for twenty-one years, but which
" it is now proposed to violate.

" When, on various occasions formerly,
" attempts were made by some parties among
" Protestants to introduce for their purposes,
" such a modification of the system as

" would have amounted to a subversion of
" it, I always strenuously opposed any such
" unwarrantable changes. I never would,
" nor ever will, consent to break faith either
" with Roman Catholics or with Protestants.

" And that the recent proceedings of the
" Board (even if not followed up—and I
" cannot doubt they will be by further steps
" in the same direction) do amount to a
" breach of faith with the public, and involve
" a misapplication of the public money, is a
" conclusion which appears perfectly evident
" both to myself and to all those confidential
" advisers, including some of the ablest
" and most upright characters in existence,
" with whom I have discussed the subject.

" I will take the liberty of suggesting, in
" conclusion—not as a Commissioner, but
" as a patron of a national school—that
" measures should be taken to secure at least
" the schools (amounting to several hundreds)
" which are actually using the books proposed
" to be discarded, from being deprived of
" the advantage they have hitherto enjoyed.
" The patrons of those schools, if thus
" grievously wronged, will be likely to bring

" forward their complaints in a manner which
" may lead to such contests as are much to
" be deprecated."

(Signed) "RD. DUBLIN."

The ex-Lord Chancellor Blackburne and
Mr. Baron Greene took the same view as
Dr. Whately, and withdrew with the books
from the Board.

Lord St. Germans wrote to Dr. Whately
expressive of his regret at the retirement of
three Commissioners so efficient and influential, but totally dissenting from the conclusions at which they had arrived.

" The Board, wrote his Excellency, has
" resolved that a particular religious book,
" which many Roman Catholics, lay as
" well as clerical, declare that they con-
" scientiously disapproved, shall be no longer
" used in any national school. It is true
" that this book formerly received the una-
" nimous sanction of the Commissioners;
" but it is no less true that all the Roman
" Catholic Commissioners who now have
" seats at the Board protest against its
" use. It is, they say, an essentially Pro-

" testant work; inconsistent with the doc-
" trines of the Roman Catholic Church.
" They cannot, as members of that Church,
" continue to sanction, still less can they
" compel Catholic teachers to use it in the
" schools. The exclusion of this book at the
" time of combined instruction cannot then
" I think be looked upon by any patron as a
" breach of faith or as the violation of a
" compact. I must further observe that a
" body which has legal power to authorize
" the use of a book, must, in my opinion, not
" only have a legal power, but also fair and
" capable right to prohibit its use on good
" and sufficient grounds. The fact, that no
" book can be introduced without the sanc-
" tion of every Commissioner, does not
" appear to prove that a book once introduced
" must be retained for ever, even though a
" majority of the Commissioners are of
" opinion that it ought to be withdrawn."

The Archbishop wrote a rejoinder, marked
" private," in which he vigorously attacked
the opinions of the Lord Lieutenant expressed
in the foregoing passages, strenuously denying
the right of the Commissioners to withdraw

books once sanctioned. "And if I had con-
" tended," he said,   .

" That this was no breach of faith with the
" public, I should have forfeited from hence-
" forth all claim to confidence in my upright-
" ness, not only in what regards the schools,
" but in all my other transactions. I add,
" that all persons have now reason to fear
" not only unlimited encroachments on the
" system made by the Commissioners them-
" selves directly, but also their ratifying the
" encroachments made without their autho-
" rity by persons who had no shadow of right
" to take such steps. In fact it is to these
" irregular proceedings in some of the model
" schools (and which were subsequently
" approved and confirmed) that the present
" unhappy state of things is chiefly to be
" traced."

The Viceroy continued proof against Dr.
Whately's logic, which had now admittedly
failed, as well as the plan that it aimed to
prop. Alluding to some incredulous persons
—though, we believe, not on this occasion—
Dr. Whately said :—

" To attempt to convince some men, by

" even the strongest reasons and most cogent
" arguments, would be like King Lear putting
" a letter before a man without eyes, and
" saying, 'Mark but the penning of it;' to
" which he answers, 'Were all the letters
" ' suns, I could not see one.' "

Lord St. Germans simply stated that the
only question which he had to consider was
whether the circumstances of the case submitted to him by the Archbishop, were such
as would justify him in displacing the majority of the Board, and appointing other
persons to be Commissioners in their room,
and he thought they were not.

Dr. Whately seems to have been warm in
communicating the fact of his retirement to
the Board; for that body on the 12th August,
1853, passed a resolution expressive of their
" deep regret that his Grace had used language
" which they are compelled to pronounce to
" be unjustifiable and unbecoming."

The contest continued to rage; the very
existence of the National Board was at stake.
At length the charges preferred by Dr.
Whately went for investigation before the
House of Lords, when a mass of conflicting

evidence transpired. The Archbishop and Mr. Blackburne reiterated their charges against the Board; other witnesses gave strong evidence on both sides, and it is a curious fact that while some of those who expressed themselves favourable to the system have since utterly modified their views, more than one who bore strong testimony against it have become its ardent supporters. A remarkable instance of this change of feeling is found in the case of Dr. Verschoyle, ex-Honorary Secretary to the Church Education Society, and now Bishop of Kilmore, who, from being an active opponent of the national system, and a strong witness against it, has since advocated the question with considerable warmth.

Dr. Whately was examined at considerable length :—

" *Chairman.*—I believe your Grace was one " of the original members of the Board of " Education in Ireland ? "

" I was ! "

" You resigned your seat at the Board last " year ? "

" I ceased to be a Commissioner last year !
" I do not like to use the word ' resigned.' "

" *Lord Ardrossan.*—Have you taken a very
" warm interest in the system from the com-
" mencement ? "

" From the very commencement I have.
" It was proposed to me first in the month
" of November after my appointment, and I
" laboured to make myself fully master of
" the system, and of the circumstances that
" might affect the carrying of it out, and I
" laboured most assiduously ever after. I
" was not merely an attendant at the weekly
" meetings of the Board, but I was in the
" course of the week a very frequent attend-
" ant at the model school; and conferred
" with the other Commissioners in private,
" and with the inspectors and schoolmasters,
" and other officers that were concerned in
" carrying on the system. So that, in fact,
" I devoted a great deal more time and at-
" tention to it than merely as an attendant
" at the ordinary weekly meetings of the
" Board. I have taken the liberty of men-
" tioning that circumstance for this reason,
" that there was a pamphlet brought out

" some years afterwards by a person who
" stated distinctly that Provost Sadleir and
" myself seldom or never attended the
" meetings of the Board, and knew nothing
" of what was going on, but merely signed,
" without examination, any papers that were
" put before us; which was a statement that
" perhaps he might not have known to be
" untrue, but if he had made the slightest
" inquiry, he might have ascertained that it
" was the very reverse of the truth."

" Will you be kind enough to state to the
" Committee how the combined religious
" instruction was first engrafted on the
" system ? "

" It was at a very early meeting of the
" Commissioners, at which it was suggested
" by some of them—a suggestion immediately
" adopted by the others—that it would be
" a thing most unacceptable, and indeed
" almost impossible to be carried on, to
" ignore altogether everything connected
" with religion ; that it would be possible to
" have an *anti*-religious system ; that is to
" say, we might have just such an education
" in reference to Christianity, as we are

" accustomed always to give, in reference
" to the heathen religions, to all young
" gentlemen who have a classical education.
" We teach them, and we could not avoid
" teaching them, that there were such beings
" worshipped as Jupiter and Neptune. We
" teach them that all this heathen mythology
" which they are obliged to learn, in order to
" understand the history and geography of
" ancient nations, was all a delusion, all
" untrue and unworthy of attention, except
" for the sake of elucidating the authors
" which they are reading. For it would be
" impossible to give a young man what is
" called a classical education, and to ignore
" altogether the existence of any such thing
" as the heathen mythology. And we agreed
" accordingly, that, though it would be pos-
" sible to give an anti-religious education,
" and to teach that Christianity and Mahom-
" medanism and Paganism are all systems
" of delusion, it would be impossible to
" ignore (as the modern phrase is) all
" reference to religion, unless we were con-
" tented with simply teaching the children to
" read and write, which might be done out

" of Æsop's Fables. Accordingly, it was
" suggested that the plan should be so far
" modified, that everything which could be
" agreed upon by the Commissioners, as
" being something unexceptionable for Chris-
" tians of all denominations, should be in-
" troduced in the various lessons on history
" and geography, and in whatever other ways
" might seem most suitable. And in addition
" to this, Dr. Carlile, who was one of the
" original Commissioners, suggested that a
" considerable portion of Scripture might be
" introduced, not enforced, but recommended
" by the Commissioners, by framing a new
" version, that should not adhere rigidly
" either to the authorized version or to the
" Douay, respecting which there was a great
" deal of party spirit and controversy afloat.
" This was also acceded to by Archbishop
" Murray, and by all the other Roman
" Catholic as well as Protestant Commis-
" sioners. And accordingly he, with the
" assistance of some of the other Commis-
" sioners, prepared those lessons from the
" Scriptures that were published by the
" Board. But although the reading of those
" Scripture Lessons was never made com-

" pulsory, that is, no patron was allowed to
" compel children to read them if the parents
" objected, the Reading Books (as they were
" called) of the Board contained a great
" deal of Scripture History and frequent
" allusions to Christianity, and a proper
" mixture of religious motives, addressed to
" Christians as such in all the moral lessons
" given; and those books the patrons of any
" school may *require* the children who attend
" the school to read."

Some of the ablest heads measured their
strength together and pitted themselves
determinedly. It was a great contest,
strenuously maintained on both sides, and
after lasting for four months, it was a
drawn battle, for their Lordships could not
agree to a report.

A digest of the Parliamentary evidence,
nominally compiled by the late Mr. Cross, but
chiefly the work of Dr. Whately, who paid all
expenses of getting it through the press, was
published by Groombridge; and propping
pamphlets—inspired by his Grace—appeared
from the pen of Dr. Cooke Taylor, who had
been at one time almost an inmate of the
Palace.

The Archbishop was examined chiefly by Lord Ardrossan and Dr. Knox, Bishop of Down, then a short time only appointed to his see. In allusion to this appointment—in some quarters unpopular—Dr. Whately made a good pun, and a still better stroke of wit. " The Irish Government," he said, " will not " be able to stand many more such *Knocks* " *Down* as this." The friends of the same prelate—and we are bound to add that they are not few—enumerated his merits in reply to this satire, and mentioned, among other claims, that Dr. Knox had compiled an excellent Ecclesiastical Directory, with the value of livings. " If that be so," muttered his Grace, " I hope that next time the " claims of our friend Thom will not be over-" looked."

English readers may be reminded that Mr. Thom is the compiler of the well-known " Dublin Directory." As the publisher of the National school-books he was brought into familiar relations with Dr. Whately.

Lord Macaulay tells us that the Highland chiefs were never known to act together effectively except under the command of a

stranger. The remark does not apply to the
Irish bishops under the command of a Saxon
Metropolitan. No cordiality or co-operation
ever subsisted between Archbishop Whately
and the many prelates who since 1831 have
officiated in Ireland, the recently appointed
Bishop of Killaloe, his former secretary and
chaplain, of course excepted. Another ex-
Chaplain, the present Bishop of Meath, has
strongly dissented, in his episcopal capacity,
from the policy of Dr. Whately, and failed
even to attend his funeral.

The use of a little volume of " Sacred
" Poetry " was relinquished by the Roman
Catholic children at the same time as the
other books. It was mainly compiled by Dr.
Whately, though nominally edited by a lady
inmate of the palace; and included, with
some original pieces, a selection from the
best hymns of Watts and others. Some of
them are versified passages from the Douay
version. " Give me but the ballad-singers,
" and I will revolutionize the country," says
Voltaire. " I would give the making of the
" laws for the making of the ballads of the
" people," remarked the great Chatham. It

has been alleged that Dr. Whately, by placing these and other peculiarly planned volumes in the hands of the people, aimed to revolutionize the religious and political mind of Ireland. The hymns were of a searchingly religious character. " A well-composed song," says the first Napoleon, " strikes and softens " the mind, and produces a greater effect " than a moral work which convinces our " reason, but does not warm our feelings, nor " affect the slightest alteration in our habits."

The preface to " The Sacred Poetry " assigned loftier reasons for its compilation. " The practice of throwing important truths " and precepts into a poetical form, for the " purpose of being committed to memory, " has prevailed in all nations that have made " any advancement towards civilization or " refinement. It is a practice that comes " commended to us by the example of the " inspired writers ; for a considerable portion " of the Sacred Scriptures consists of poems, " embodying in them the leading events of " history, and the great fundamental doctrines " and precepts of religion.

" Poetry of this description, committed to

" memory, becomes a record of facts and of
" precepts, which a man carries constantly
" about with him, ready to be used for his
" direction when he may require it. The
" poetical form, also, into which sacred truths
" and precepts have thus been moulded, tends
" to soften his manners, to refine his taste,
" and to give him a relish for pleasures of a
" higher order and of a purer kind than those
" to which he might otherwise be tempted to
" betake himself."

Some of the hymns introduced were calculated to catch the Catholic fancy. Take for
example this Hymn of the B. V. Mary :—

LUKE I. 46—55.

1 My soul and spirit, filled with joy,
   My God my Saviour praise,
   Whose goodness did from poor estate
   His humble handmaid raise.

2 Me blessed of God, the God of might,
   All ages shall proclaim ;
   From age to age his mercy lasts,
   And holy is his name.

3 Strength with his arm the Almighty showed,
   The proud his looks abased :
   He cast the mighty to the ground,
   The meek to honor raised.

4 The hungry with good things were filled,
　　The rich with hunger pined :
　　He sent his servant Israel help,
　　And called his love to mind.

5 Which to our fathers' ancient race
　　His promise did ensure :
　　To Abraham and his chosen seed,
　　For ever to endure.

Dr. Whately, in one of his last charges, frankly avows the bitter disappointment and chagrin with which he never ceased to view the defeat of his plan of National Education, partly by Catholics, but largely by Protestants.

" The ultimate result, however, of this
" opposition has been the virtual suppression
" of the work—*a measure which could never*
" *have been carried but for that opposition.*
" There was neglected, and finally lost, an
" opportunity which no one could have calcu-
" lated on beforehand as likely to offer, and
" which no one can expect ever to return ;—
" a golden opportunity for diffusing among
" the great mass of the Irish people such an
" amount of Scriptural knowledge as they
" had never had hitherto, nor are ever likely
" to have hereafter."

And then referring to the statement that
" a large proportion " of Roman Catholics

were believed to deprecate " the general diffu-
" sion of Scripture knowledge " as unfavourable to their Church, he added, " With what
" alarm these persons must have seen the
" books I have been speaking of placed, with
" the sanction of rulers of their own Church,
" in the hands of hundreds of thousands of
" the youth of their communion ; and with
" what wondering exultation must they have
" seen the scheme defeated through the
" agency of Protestants ! "

Although full of poetic appreciation and
power, Dr. Whately, like Samuel Johnson,
had no ear for music ; and we are not quite
sure that he could at once recognize the
" Dead March in Saul " from " St. Patrick's
" Day." A few years ago he sent for a
popular composer, then and still a citizen of
Dublin, and expressed a desire that he should
furnish a chant within a given time. The
task was executed to the almost enthusiastic
satisfaction of the composer, whose equa-
nimity was much disturbed by the Archbishop insisting that some sacred poetry, in
the authorship of which he had an interest, should be set to the identical music
supplied.

In vain the composer endeavoured to explain that the Archbishop's lines fell short by several feet of the measure of the melody; but Dr. Whately pushed the objection aside, and peremptorily desired that they should go in unaltered. The chant, " with all its im-" perfections on its head," was subsequently often sung throughout the churches of the city; thus illustrating the virtue of canonical obedience, and, at the same time, showing that the Archbishop knew more about his mitre than his metre. Dr. Whately, however, although innocent of music, respected it as a great science—just as he respected trigonometry, of which he knew almost nothing; and when, in 1848, Jenny Lind, with her red coat and drum, took Dublin by storm, the Archbishop showed the Daughter of the Regiment considerable attention, and invited her to his house.

The Archbishop was, as we have said, fond of poetry, but he far from moulded his style upon a study of the British Poets. " Learn-" ing a language from its poets," he said, " is like studying botany in a garden of " double flowers." And of poetry he pithily said " that it was imitative of prose, in the

" same manner as singing of ordinary speak-
" ing, and dancing of ordinary action."
We know of but one attempt at versifica-
tion on the part of Dr. Whately—an epi-
gram, stinging as well as ringing. The following parody on a nursery jingle, and written in satiric allusion to Dr. Wordsworth's
well-known volume, " Who wrote *Icon Basi-*
" *likè*," has been attributed to Dr. Whately.*

> " Who wrote 'Who wrote Icon Basilikè?'
> " ' I,' said the Master of Trinity,
> " I, with my little Divinity,
> " I wrote ' Who wrote Icon Basilikè?' "

Other versions make the third line read
" *I, with my small ability*," and, as some
think, for the better.

But to return to the Education question :

> " Between two stools, we can't forget,
> " A man may often be upset,"

was well illustrated in Dr. Whately's downfall from his pedestal in Tyrone House. Archbishop Cullen, in a public letter addressed to
the writer of these pages, and dated 15th

---

* " Notes and Queries," 2nd S. No. 69, p. 339.

December, 1860, summarizes some views which had been already more fully un-folded.

" When Lord Stanley first proposed the " mixed system, Catholics were solemnly " assured that under it their children would " be free from the remotest danger of prosely-" tism, and it was understood that the action " of Government should be restricted to the " giving of aid to schools, and to inspection " as to the application of the funds and the " literary progress of the children.

" But those flattering promises have not " been realized. The safeguards laid down " by Lord Stanley have been gradually with-" drawn ; Catholic children are now publicly " receiving religious instruction from Pro-" testant teachers ; books replete with an " anti-Catholic spirit, and compiled from Pro-" testant sources, under the direction of a " rationalistic dignitary of the Protestant " Establishment, the author of a work en-" titled ' Errors of Romanism,' have been " published at the public expense, and intro-" duced into the schools for the use of Catho-" lic children ; model and training mixed " schools have been established, well calcu-

" lated to inspire the future masters and
" mistresses of the country with indifference
" to every creed, and to throw into the hands
" of Government officials, in a most uncon-
" stitutional manner, equally dangerous to
" religion and society, the education of the
" rising Catholic generation of Ireland, by
" committing to their officials the formation
" of future masters."

Many members of the Protestant and Dissenting clergy expressed themselves in still
stronger language against the system. The
Rev. Dr. Cooke opines :—

" 1. It was invented and imposed, not at
" the wish of Protestants, but to please the
" priests of Rome in their dislike to Bible-
" reading in schools. 2. During four hours
" every day the Bible must be excluded, and
" to read it during that time would forfeit
" all assistance. 3. During four hours a
" day neither schoolmaster nor minister dare
" pray in the school, under the above penalty.
" 4. No minister dare ever preach in the
" school, under like penalty. 5. The Romish
" priest is a visitor of the school, whether
" the committee will or not, and can turn
" out the Protestant children one day every

" week in the year to teach that Protest-
" ants are heretics, and cannot as such be
" saved, being out of the pale of the Church.
" 6. The Board publishes books that incul-
" cate Popery, and authorizes their use in
" schools.   7. The Board has published in
" one of their school-books, a well-known
" seditious song, called *Erin-Go-Bragh*, and
" gives it among their schools."

It was complained, on the other hand, by
a democratic leader, that the " Poetic Ex-
" tracts," as published by the Commissioners,
tended to denationalize the popular mind,
inasmuch as Scott's beautiful lines,   .

> " Breathes there a man with soul so dead
> Who never to himself hath said—
> This is my own—my native land ! "

escaped the vigilance of the original compiler ;
but though applying to no particular country,
it was expunged from subsequent editions,
lest the youth of Ireland should imbibe a
national thought.

We fear it cannot be said of Dr. Whately
as of the Geraldines, " Ipsis Hibernis Hiber-
" nior."   In 1846 a new edition of the books
used in the National Schools was prepared

under the supervision of the Archbishop. Until that year there had been included in the selections for reading lessons, "The Exile " of Erin," by Campbell; "Lines, by Miss " Balfour, to the Irish Harp Society," a " Description of the Lakes of Killarney," of the " Giant's Causeway," and other similar pieces; but, together with " The Downfall " of Poland," they were all expurgated from the new edition. The masters were strictly prohibited from referring in the presence of the pupils to any of the past glories of Irish history; and thus every means were employed to emasculate the national mind of Ireland.

For years Dr. Whately practically pursued this policy with, as usual, his eyes wide open.

" It is a great mistake," he said, " often " made in practice, if not in theory, to sup- " pose that a child's character, intellectual and " moral, is formed by those books only which " we put into his hands with that *design*. " As hardly anything can accidentally touch " the soft clay without stamping its mark on " it, so hardly any reading can interest a

" child, without contributing in some degree,
" though the book itself be afterwards totally
" forgotten, to form the character; and the
" parents, therefore, who, merely requiring
" from him a certain course of *study*, pay
" little or no attention to story-books, are
" educating him they know not how."

In this view Dr. Whately would seem to
have perfectly concurred with Thomas Davis,
one of the clearest thinkers of the Young
Ireland party; but the concurrence was
unconscious and accidental.

Davis bemoaned that of the early Fathers
and Missionaries of the Irish Church—a
numerous and glorious host—we have no
popular histories, and that our accounts of
the great Irishmen of the middle and subsequent ages were few and most unsatisfac-
tory. " The influence on the young mind
" of Ireland of such books," he adds, " would
" be incalculably great. Boys who read of
" their own will, as most Irish boys do, read
" intently. They build and plant with
" Robinson Crusoe; they plot and re-plot
" with Baron Trenck; they are edified and
" instructed with Sandford and Merton;

" they are loyalists with Falkland, and pa-
" triots with Lord Edward. The writer of
" books popular among boys may calculate
" on revolutionizing a country at the out-
" side in thirty years." Davis also indicated
the tendency which such books would possess to teach Ireland self-respect and self-
reliance : " But it would have another effect.
" It would save our men—our speakers and
" writers — from the constantly recurring
" disgrace of quoting foreign names as illus-
" trative of patriotism, acquirement, or
" virtue. It would furnish them with ac-
" counts of Irish worthies as honest as
" Aristides, as pure as Scipio, as wise as
" Fabius, as brave as Cæsar, as eloquent as
" Tully. It would save them the labour and
" the seeming pedantry of flying for ever to
" Greece and Rome for their examples and
" instances. This second advantage would
" be hardly inferior to the first. It would
" create Irish synonyms * for every virtue
. " and every endowment."

" From generation to generation," he in-

* Dr. Whately preferred English Synonyms. *Vide*
his book on the subject.

dignantly concluded, " the weeds and briars
" of negligence, fed on the damps and dark-
" ness of night, have been suffered to rankle
" about the graves of our great predecessors.
" Let a general clearance be proclaimed,
" and let all the earnest and honest among
" the living join in justification of all the
" brave and good among the dead."

Poor Davis had little more than penned
these stirring sentiments, when he himself
was summoned to join " the brave and good
" among the dead ;" but with his last breath
he continued to protest against the dena-
tionalizing influences which were being shed
upon the rising youth of Ireland. When the
author of " Breathes there a man with soul
" so dead " said " It is a mistake to suppose
" that by making men bad Scotchmen you
" make them good Englishmen," the sentiment was as applicable to Ireland as to
Scotland.

The jealous spirit that watched over
every department of their education was
curiously exhibited in 1849. A teacher of
music having introduced some numbers of
Robinson's edition of " Moore's Melodies "

into the metropolitan schools, as they con-
tain cheap classical music of a description
best adapted for his purpose, after a few
lessons, orders came forbidding their continuance.

After the death of Davis, Mr. Gavan Duffy,
in the *Nation* newspaper, perpetuated the
protest which his friend had been the first to
raise. He submitted that it was impossible
to rear a nation to its full stature upon
foreign thought, and asked, " Was it fair
" that native shrines should be veiled before
" the eyes of the young child while he is
" taught to kneel at those of other lands ?"

The writer complained that " After going
" over all ballad history, from Homer to
" Macaulay, through north and south, east
" and west of Europe, and even crossing the
" ocean to pay a tribute to the muse of the
" native savages of America, the Education
" Commissioner had said that the national
" poetry of *Ireland* is a subject upon which
" he has left himself *no space* to make any
" remarks."

Dr. Whately was no doubt right to have
omitted, at that critical period of revolu-

tionary feeling, the bards of Young Ireland;
but there were previous poets who sang
of noble deeds and of the wild, beautiful
legends of Erin, which their verse had made
more beautiful, who might well have got a
niche. Moore, no doubt, received a place;
but the specimens were mainly, if not entirely, of his sacred poetry and "An Ode
" to a Grasshopper." The compiler of these
poetical selections gave offence to the Young
Ireland party by teaching the "Irish child to
" chant 'The Stately Homes of England.' "
And it was alleged, but somewhat illogically,
that "France might as well make ' Rule,
" ' Britannia,' her national song, in the place
" of the ' Marseillaise,' or America rear her
" youthful population upon the ' British
" ' Grenadiers.' "

In a sounder view it was added:—" Ger-
" many tried to live upon foreign thought
" for a hundred years or more—English and
" French, or any thought except their own—
" but nothing came of it. So at last, headed
" by those grand iconoclasts, Lessing, Herder,
" Jieck, Goethe, and others, they threw
" down all the foreign idols, and went back

" to drink of their own holy wells, their
" Sagas, Mährchen, and wild lays of the
" Niebelungen. There they found inspira-
" tion, and the free, native tide of thought
" has ever since poured forth in channels
" created by its own daring force—the only
" fitting channels for that wondrous German
" mind, at once the profoundest and most
" imaginative of Europe ; while, on the other
" hand, by stifling the free utterance of
" native thought, the literature of modern
" Italy has become the most meagre, because
" the least idiomatic of Europe. And is the
" censorship of genius here to equal that of
" the Austrians in Italy, where the words
" country, freedom, independence, were for-
" bidden to be uttered ? True, there is a
" magic might in song. All rulers and des-
" pots know this well. Napoleon found its
" power, when the chorus—

'Sie sollen ihn nicht haben der freie deutsche Rhein ！'

" made all Germany fly to arms for the war
" of liberation. ‘The songs of the poets be-
" ‘ come swords in the hands of the patriots,’ ”
sang the organs of Young Ireland. " Can

" it be in fear of this transmutation, that
" Irish song is not flung into the furnace
" of young hearts ?   Do they fear it will fuse
" into   metal ? these Commissioners, who
" place the poets of Ireland in the Index
" Expurgatorius ? "

There can be no doubt that Dr. Whately
entertained this fear.

The biographies of the poets form the
third volume of the work.   They are interesting, useful, and well executed,—affording
examples of acute and elegant criticism by
the best writers of the day.   Wherever the
editor speaks in his own person, it is with
taste and judgment.

National Education had a narrow escape
of incurring an irrevocable Papal censure,
near twenty years previous to its final condemnation by the Roman Catholic Bishops of
Ireland.   Propaganda had decided upon issu-
ing a formal prohibition of it in July, 1840 ;
but Archbishop Murray addressed a letter
to the Pope, begging that a Legate might
be sent to Ireland to examine, on the spot,
the constitution and working of the suspected system ; and the result was a with-

drawal. A rescript issued by authority of Gregory XVI., while permitting the Irish Catholics to avail themselves of National Education, pointed out some simple safeguards which it seemed expedient to introduce. Reasons were assigned for allowing this privilege, including " the op- " portunity the schools give for the instruc- " tion of youth—gratitude to Parliament for " granting large sums of money to schools " for the Irish people—the fear lest all the " money and influence should pass into the " hands of heterodox teachers, and espe- " cially the happy intelligence that during " the ten years in which that system was " received the Catholic religion had suffered " no injury." The Rescript further declared that Catholics might be taught by Protestants or sectaries, provided that religion, morality, or Sacred History were not included in the instruction.

It will be observed that Dr. Whately's books clashed with the latter enactment. Mixed *secular* instruction would, we believe, have been tolerated by the Holy See, which had before it the high authority of St. Jerome, who studied Hebrew under the Rabbis, a sect which denied the divinity of our Saviour.

It was whilst some of these difficulties to which we referred beset the National System of Education, that Dr. Copleston, addressing Sir Thomas Philips, said :—

" I read with much satisfaction your re-
" marks upon the system of combined
" instruction in the Irish schools. I used
" to forebode what has happened, when con-
" versing, as I often did, with my old and
" revered friend, the Archbishop of Dublin ;
" but latterly I have said nothing, because
" he is pledged to the measure ; and if,
" under his patronage, with talents and vir-
" tues greatly above the average of mankind,
" the scheme has failed, as you have clearly
" pointed out that it has, there must, I am
" sure, be something essentially wrong and
" impracticable in it."

CHAPTER VI.

In May, 1853, the Earl of Shaftesbury, having presented a petition for the registration and inspection of nunneries, Dr. Whately, from his place in Parliament, somewhat to the surprise of friends and foes, rose to " express his hearty concurrence in the " general prayer of the petition. It was his " conviction that there was wanted some " additional legislation for the personal pro- " tection of individuals. Several accusations " had been brought against him of ultra- " Liberalism, and perhaps other isms. He " wished not to advocate any restrictions " upon the liberty of Christians of any de- " nomination. He, however, thought that " Parliament was called upon to interfere, " and to pass a law not to abridge, but to " secure the liberty of individuals. He called

" upon their lordships to consider the serious
" grievance of any of our fellow-subjects
" being condemned, without a hearing, for
" the commission of any crime, to perpetual
" imprisonment or transportation for life,
" and also to consider whether it was not
" possible that those penalties might be in-
" flicted on some of our fellow-subjects with-
" out its coming to the knowledge of any
" person capable of affording redress. Now,
" suppose a young woman was received as a
" novice in some institution, and was placed
" under coercion. Her friends might have
" some suspicion about her, but on inquiry
" her existence was denied. They were told
" that nothing was known about her—or, if
" the novice were in the house, they were
" told she was too unwell to see such and
" such a person, or wished to have nothing
" more to do with them. And there were
" institutions in this island which were
" affiliated with similar institutions on the
" Continent. Therefore, as he had said,
" persons might be sentenced to undergo the
" illegal penalty, not only of imprisonment,
" but of transportation for life ; and it was

" no such impossible a thing for a person
" to be spirited away to some foreign insti-
" tution, and there for ever to be kept out
" of the sight or knowledge of his or her
" friends." *

* Dr. Whately was often quite as credulous as he was
sceptical. There can be no doubt that he was influenced
to some extent by the rhapsodies of Maria Monk ; and
possibly by the " Narrative of Six Years' Captivity and
" Sufferings among the Monks of St. Bernard, at Charn-
" wood Forest, Leicestershire," by William F. Jeffryes,
who obtained, by fraud, hospitality for two days in the
convent. He wrote in his book that the moment he
entered the monastery-gate he felt that he was a prisoner,
" like a bird shut up in a cage ; " that he was baptized
against his will, under the strange name of St. Ceil ; was
allowed no communication with friends ; was twice bled—
had his body punctured with sharp instruments ; that
during his stay, several made their escape ; that some
were overtaken, and brought back, with mouths muffled
and arms tied ; but how they were afterwards disposed
of he never could learn. The book had an enormous
circulation ; and for the hundred who read it, probably
not one ever saw a retractation from the publishers—
which concluded in the following words :—

" We, therefore, the undersigned, do hereby declare
" our deep and solemn conviction that the narrative of
" the said William F. Jeffryes is a tissue of the grossest
" and most unwarrantable falsehoods ; and we feel it our
" bounden duty to publish this statement to the world,
" as some little reparation for the injury we have been

The threatened legislation, and Dr. Whately's connection with it, excited a considerable sensation in Ireland. Aggregate meetings were held, and a formidable opposition, parliamentary and otherwise, was organized. The Roman Catholic Archbishop of Dublin published an elaborate document in reply to the speech of Dr. Whately, and in vindication of religious communities generally, and then addressing his flock, he said :—

"You are well acquainted with the ser-
" vices rendered by them to the deaf and
" the mute, the orphan and the widow : you
" know that they afford an asylum to many
" unprotected females, whom, preserved from
" the contagion of vice, they instruct in the
" arts of domestic life, and prepare to be
" useful members of society. But, passing

" the innocent means of inflicting on the community of
" Mount St. Bernard.

" (Signed)　　　" W. S. NAYLER.
" THOMAS RAGG."

The registries of Stafford gaol record that the author was, on 30th June, 1849, committed, as a "rogue and a " vagabond," for three months with hard labour.

" all these things over in silence, what shall
" we say of their successful labours in the
" cause of education ? Their seminaries for
" the instruction of the higher classes can
" compete with similar establishments in any
" country, and are esteemed and encouraged
" by all the Catholic families in the kingdom.
" The sacrifices they have made and are
" daily making to give a good, religious, and
" literary education to the children of the
" poor, are above all praise ; without fear of
" being contradicted, we may assert, that
" the modesty, the purity, the attachment to
" religion, and the many other virtues which
" distinguish and adorn the females of Ire-
" land, are due under Heaven to the zeal,
" and piety, and good example of our reli-
" gious communities. Is it not, then, a
" matter of great glory to the people of
" Ireland, to reflect that in the midst of their
" poverty and wretchedness, they have been
" able to found such institutions and to bring
" them to perfection ? "

In reply to the assertion that the ladies
were cruelly detained within the convent
walls against their will, Dr. Cullen, who had

himself no less than fifteen sisters, cousins, and nieces, nuns, submitted—

" 1stly. That the greatest possible care is
" taken to give all candidates a full know-
" ledge of a religious life and its duties, and
" that they are not admitted to holy profes-
" sion until they have served a noviciate and
" a period of probation, which oftentimes
" are extended over three years.

" 2ndly. That it is strictly prescribed that
" no one shall be professed unless previously
" examined by the bishop of the diocese or
" his deputy.

" 3rdly. That the severest censures of the
" Church are fulminated against those who
" would sacrilegiously pretend to force any
" one to become a religious against her will.
" And,

" 4thly. That, even after profession, per-
" mission to retire is sometimes granted.
" Such cases are rare, because the force of
" conscience is powerful with the true chil-
" dren of God, and because the greatest pre-
" cautions are taken by the Catholic Church
" to preserve the liberty of the individual
" before profession; but the occasional re-

" laxations referred to show how little
" disposition there is on the part of the
" Church to exercise coercion or restraint.
" However, omitting all these considerations,
" let me ask, does the author of this charge
" forget that the convents are in the middle
" of our most populous towns and cities;
" that their doors are open to all; and that,
" if any of the inmates think fit to leave
" their retirement, they are protected in
" doing so by the laws of their country?
" This gentleman perhaps thinks that it
" must be an intolerable burthen to crucify
" one's own flesh, with its vices and concu-
" piscences, and to lead a holy life in the
" shade of the sanctuary, far from the tur-
" moil of the world."

Dr. Cullen, without directly avowing it,
aimed to rouse the laity to resistance. He
said that a serious charge was levelled against
them.

" Are they not reproached with being
" like the Pagans condemned by St. Paul
" for the want of affection? For, if what is
" stated be true, that is, if the religious in
" the convents be incarcerated, and detained

" against their will, it must necessarily follow
" that their parents, their brothers, and
" sisters are devoid of all feelings of affec-
" tion, and have coolly submitted to see
" their relatives detained in prison and
" oppressed, leaving the task of raising his
" voice in their favour, and of calling for
" their liberation, to the principal Protestant
" dignitary in this city."

A hurricane was raised,* in the midst of

---

* The Roman Catholic nobility of England published
a protest, concluding with :—"Lastly, the undersigned
" declare that it is morally impossible that cases of un-
" lawful imprisonment or physical restraints on liberty
" should exist in convents without the fact being known
" to them and their families. Any assumption of such
" cases directly inculpates them, as neglectful of their
" first duties, as men and Christians, and as participators
" in the wrongful detention of those whom by every tie
" of kindred and honour, they were called on to protect;
" and therefore, that the present bill, by countenancing
" the false and injurious suspicions of ignorant and pre-
" judiced persons, that inmates of convents are subject to
" unlawful imprisonment, is a libellous insult to the
" ladies in question, to their families, and to the under-
" signed."

This document was signed by Lords Arundel and
Surrey, E. Fitzallan Howard, Feilding, Camoys, Stourton,
Vaux of Harrowden, Petre, Stafford, Lovat, Dormer,
and many others.

which Dr. Whately, for the first time in his life, hid his head; and Lord Shaftesbury's bill was blown even higher than the flights of his own imagination. Pending this consummation, a Catholic gentleman, who had been intimately associated with the Archbishop as a Commissioner of National Education, felt and expressed a considerable feeling of regret that his Grace should have lent sanction to the bill, and enclosed to Dr. Whately a letter written by the Commissioner's sister, a nun, in which she assures her brother of the joy which filled every minute of her life; and as an excuse for not oftener writing home, describes the uninterrupted round of corporal works of mercy—prescribed rather by her own philanthropic impulses than by the rule of her order—which the longest day seemed too short to master. The letter was thrown off in the fulness of sisterly confidence, and without a thought that any eyes save her brother's should see it. Archbishop Whately seemed favourably impressed by this letter, and returned it to the lady's brother in a communication which fills four large pages of manuscript. In this remarkable letter he takes infinite pains in trying to convince him that he was guiltless of any *attack* upon Roman Catholic convents. And Dr. Whately transcribes, at great length, the softening, and to some extent qualifying portions of the speech in which he had supported Lord Shaftesbury's bill. Much of this, it would appear, had not been reported. " It " was quite unnecessary," he said, alluding to his correspondent's argumentative letter, " it was quite unnecessary to confirm what " required no confirmation ;" and he adds, " it is you and your co-religionists who have " been misled—not I." On principle he wished all institutions to be open to official visitation. The Archbishop in this letter mentioned that he was guardian of an orphan society on the Circular Road, Dublin, as well as of other institutions, in which he took a true paternal interest ; and he declared that these were the first which he should make subject to official visitation.

It is very possible that the Archbishop's public policy in reference to the Nunneries Bill was merely thrown as a sop to the Cerberus of Calvinism. Privately, Dr. Whately

continued to prove, by numberless small
traits, his great liberality.*   If not *infra dig.*
to descend from the study to the kitchen, we
may mention that his cook was obliged about
this time to resign her situation, until an illness which had obstinately clung to her
should so far abate as to enable her once
more to resume the manipulation of the
rolling-pin and basting-spoon. The medical
treatment failed, and the woman, who was a
Protestant, at length yielded to the entreaties
of a Roman Catholic relative, by soliciting

---

* Dr. Whately's objection to convents was not
because they were Roman Catholic. " In 1853," remarks an influential journal, " Mr. W. G. Cookesley,
" one of the masters of Eton school, thought fit to
" address Archbishop Whately on the enormities of Miss
" Sellon's High Church House of Mercy at Devonport.
" Mr. Cookesley in Buckinghamshire, and the Arch-
" bishop in Ireland, had no more business to interfere
" with the working of an institution in Devonshire,
" which was supported by the bishop of the diocese, and
" with which they were not in any way connected, than
" with the King of Ashantee. The Archbishop, of
" course, wrote back to Mr. Cookesley to the effect that
" he did Miss Sellon the honour of disapproving of her
" High Church opinions and practices."—*Morning Post*,
No. 28,022.

the prayers and spiritual aid of a Passionist monk, who, in connection with the object of her visit, gave her a reliquary blessed by the Pope. The woman immediately recovered, and she attributed her cure entirely to the friar, who considered that the most graceful thanksgiving in her power to render was to embrace the Roman Catholic faith. Having done so, she waited on Dr. Whately for some wages due, and not without considerable misgiving as to the result of the temerity of which she was conscious. She told all that had taken place, including her faith in relics, which, by the way, is not prescribed as an article of faith by Rome. To her surprise, the Archbishop neither laughed at nor censured her. " Holding the office which I fill," he said, "it is impossible that I can take you " back; but I have no objection to give you " a pension of ten pounds a year to the end " of your life."

Although an opponent of the practice of deducing rules of conduct from insulated texts, interpreted without reference to the general tone of Scripture, we find Dr. Whately, nevertheless, about this time, straining the

application of a verse which really has no
bearing on the question to the efforts of
Messrs. Crowder and Maynard to procure a
repeal of the law which prohibits marriage
with a sister-in-law, and so gave his vote in
favour of them.

Dr. Whately does not seem to have been
favourable to polemical encounters, though
how capable he was of maintaining an animated controversy we have had abundant
means of judging. He was much of opinion—
at least during twenty years of his reign in
Ireland, and the following curious scene belongs to that period—that the character of the
Christian religion is peace, and the end of it
to establish peace and good-will upon earth,
as the means of fitting men for heaven—an
end announced by the angels at Bethlehem,
and repeated by our Lord Jesus when about
to return to His Father: "My peace I leave
" you ; my peace I give you."

Many raw curates, hot from the mint of
Dublin University, impelled by mingled motives
of ecclesiastical ambition and undisciplined
religious zeal, would often express to the
Archbishop a strong desire of challenging to

mortal combat any number of Roman Catholic theologians, from Father Maguire and the entire College of Maynooth, to an Œcumenical Council, or even the Pope himself.

But Dr. Whately was so thoroughly averse to controversy, that he inhibited from preaching the famous polemic, Dr. Thresham Gregg, who had challenged and encountered Father Maguire.

At a dinner given to the clergy by his Grace several years ago, a renewed attempt was made by some of the more zealous clerics, to obtain the Archbishop's sanction of, and if possible his co-operation with, a Preaching Mission through Ireland, for the promotion of proselytism. " There are " difficulties," he said, " which, in the event " of your embarking in such an enterprise, " you would have to encounter. Will you " allow me to test in a way of my own your " capability for the task ? "

The proposal was hailed by an eager and unanimous response of acquiescence. " Go," he said, addressing one of the chaplains, " and bring from my study table a written " paper which you will find upon my desk. " I wish," proceeded the Archbishop after a due interval of suspense on the part of the clergy present, " I wish to personate* the " parish priest of — say — Bullyshanduffe, " where, for argument sake, we shall assume " that you will pitch your camp, preparatory " to striking the first blow. In the paper " which I am about to read for you I " shall say no more than any clergyman of " ordinary theological acquirements and a " fair knowledge of logic might be expected " to express." Dr. Whately, having swallowed a " solid glass of priestly port,"

* Arguments based upon "personation" were not unfrequent in the controversial contests which took place, previous to emancipation, between Catholic and Protestant disputants. At Carlow, the Rev. Robert Daly, now Bishop of Cashel, the Rev. Thomas Pope, the Hon. and Rev. Dr. Wingfield, and others, met on the polemical arena Rev. William Kinsella, afterwards Roman Catholic Bishop of Ossory, the Rev. James Maher, Rev. W. Clowry, and Rev. Dr. M'Sweeney. The latter, towards the close of the proceedings, which lasted three days, said :—
" 'I choose to personate a Socinian : how will you " ' convince me, upon your own principles, of the divinity " ' of the Saviour ? "The Father is greater than I." ' " Some noise and confusion ensued. The chairman was " appealed to as to whether Dr. M'Sweeney's opponents " had answered the question, and the chairman declined " to offer any opinion."—*Report*, p. 126.

and cleared his throat by a preliminary
" hem," commenced the parish priest's mis-
sive — one characterized, as we are assured,
by singular moderation, yet strikingly argumentative.

" I do not remember," observes our informant, " the various points in detail with
" which the Archbishop filled this extraor-
" dinary paper, but I specially recollect that
" he cited from the 29th to the 31st verses of
" the eighth chapter of the Acts, which
" describes Philip—prompted by the Holy
" Spirit—asking the great man of Ethiopia
" who was reading Esaias, whether he under-
" stood what he read; 'And he said, How can
" ' I, unless some man should guide me ? '
" ' Now,' proceeded Dr. Whately, ' if that
" ' man had been a Protestant, you must
" ' know as well as I do, that he would have
" ' made no such reply.' " *

* " 27 And he arose and went : and, behold, a man
" of Ethiopia, an eunuch of great authority under Can-
" dace queen of the Ethiopians, who had the charge of
" all her treasure, and had come to Jerusalem for to
" worship,

" 28 Was returning, and sitting in his chariot read
" Esaias the prophet.

There were no pears peeled or walnuts crushed during the delivery of this strange address, which furnished to the polemically disposed not a few tough morsels for digestion. As soon as Dr. Whately had concluded, an old clergyman, who had distinguished himself as an able general in the Proselytizing Crusade, when under the commandership of Archbishop Magee, rose from the foot of

" 29 Then the Spirit said unto Philip, Go near, and " join thyself to this chariot.

" 30 And Philip ran thither to *him*, and heard him " read the prophet Esaias, and said, Understandest thou " what thou readest?

" 31 And he said, How can I, except some man should " guide me? And he desired Philip that he would come " up and sit with him.

" 32 The place of the scripture which he read was " this, He was led as a sheep to the slaughter ; and like " a lamb dumb before his shearer, so opened he not his " mouth." — *Holy Bible* (authorized version), Acts, chap. viii.

In the Douay version the point does not appear so strongly. The words there employed are, "unless some " man shew me ;" the Protestant version is, "unless " some man guide me." The Douay Bible has no note upon this passage ; and we are not aware that any of the Catholic controversialists ever thought of making the point.

the table :—" Your Grace," he said, " am I
" at liberty to make an observation?"

" By all means, Mr. ——."

" I hope," he went on to say, " that your
" Grace has devoted the same amount of learn-
" ing and labour to providing an answer."

" That task, gentlemen, I have left for
" you," replied the Archbishop, glancing
round the table.

" I consider that document a most dan-
" gerous one," continued the old cleric, " and
" if the arguments which your Grace has so
" astutely put, got into the hands of the
" Roman Catholics, they might be productive
" of very mischievous results."

" It is especially those mischievous con-
" sequences which I am anxious to guard
" against," replied Dr. Whately. " The
" Schoolmaster is abroad, and you may be
" certain that your points would be met by
" these and many others still more pointed."

" I never heard anything more ingenious,"
remarked Mr. B—— L—— G——, the only
layman but one present; " The 'Historic
" Doubts' are nothing to it; and if your
" Grace consents to print it, with such a

" reply as you alone could furnish, I trust
" you will allow me to print and distribute
" fifty thousand copies of it at my own
" expense."

The Archbishop, however, laughingly insisted upon the polemically disposed clerics
present furnishing the reply, which does not
appear to have been then or since forthcoming.

Dr. Whately's dislike to religious controversy has been exhibited by all his chaplains
who have obtained sees. Bishop Fitzgerald's
inexorable attitude on the subject raised such
a storm among the Evangelicals in Cork that
he left the place. Dr. Dickenson, when
Bishop of Meath, wrote a letter, in which he
said :—

" The fact is, all persons assemble to such
" a discussion, not to investigate truth, but
" to witness a battle; and they come with a
" feeling of honour, arranging themselves on
" the side of their own champion, and hoping
" he may be victorious."

It is hardly necessary to observe that " the
" Irish Church Missions to Roman Catholics "
were begun without Dr. Whately's counsel

and continued without his co-operation.
Nevertheless he fulminated no anathema
against them, beyond a general deprecation
of the system, and a stern protest against
the abuses in which it was rich.   The present
Dean of St. Patrick's, Dr. West, when acting
as Archdeacon of Dublin, embodied in a
letter, written at Dr. Whately's instance, a
number of charges against the Irish Church
Mission Society.   To these charges Mr.
Eade in an unpublished correspondence replied.   Some of the more ardent actors in
the movement, possibly bearing in mind the
Archbishop's personation in private of a
Catholic priest, who had confessedly the best
of the argument, were so ill-advised as to
pay Protestants to personate, in public dis-
cussions, Roman Catholics, who of course got
the worst of the argument. The Rev. George
Webster, Chancellor of Cork, Rector of St.
Nicholas, and formerly curate to Dr. West,
for many years the private secretary and
confidential friend of Archbishop Whately,
reveals some curious details on this point.
Mr. Webster having detected some public
instances of personation, reported them to

the Archbishop, who at once ordered an investigation.

" On the day of the trial," writes the Rev. George Webster, " it will be seen, that one " witness deposed he saw the clergyman to " whom I alluded, paying the person who " personated the Roman Catholic; and of " this my informant said, ' *They* (Mr. Dallas " ' and his friends) *disclaimed all knowledge of* " ' *what happened two years ago, and offered no*˙ " ' *apology.*' My informant also testifies that " the clergyman of whom I complained had " been, by the Archbishop's account, brought " before his Grace at some time previous to " the investigation. The Archbishop acquits " the clergyman to whose conduct Mr. Dallas " alluded, although his Grace thinks ' it was " ' *imprudent* to allow any money to pass, as " ' being likely to create suspicions.' Here, " then, are the two cases that came definitely " to my knowledge of ordained agents who " paid persons to act the part of Roman " Catholics.

" It is very hard to believe that only two " instances of the kind that could possibly " be adduced, if one knew all that has been " done in Ireland since the I. C. M. began,

" were just the two that came to my know-
" ledge, although I never paid the least
" attention to the operations of the *Irish*
" *Church Missions* outside my own parish."

Dr. Whately called upon the Rev. Mr.
Dallas, Secretary to the Irish Church
Mission Society, for an explanation of the
particular instance in question. "The ex-
" planation" having been furnished, the
Archbishop thus wrote :—

"Dublin, 20*th Nov.*, 1857.

" My dear Sir,—

"You have given a satisfactory ex-
" planation of the transaction relative to the
" money given to one of the attendants on
" the controversial classes. And, though it
" was an *imprudent* thing to let any money
" pass, as being likely to create suspicions,
" you must not imagine that I ever myself
" suspected the society of keeping pre-
" tended controversialists in pay, much
" less that any such notion had any
" share in influencing my decision. But,
" waiving further reference to the several
" complaints which I investigated, and as-
" suming that all of them were satisfactorily

" answered as that one (*which, however, is*
" *beyond what I am prepared to admit*),* still
" the main consideration that influenced me
" was the absence of all proof of any positive
" *good* results. It was all hopes for an
" uncertain future; while, for the present,
" there was the uncompensated evil of much
" acrimonious feeling, excluding (as the
" curates and several of the inhabitants
" testified) those quieter approaches of good
" which had formerly existed. The parochial
" clergy, to whom was *committed* the *spiritua-*
" *charge* of the district, and who are solemnly
" bound to act therein according to the best
" of their own judgment, and whom I have
" no reason to suspect of want of anxiety for
" its Christian welfare, thought that the
" *burden of proof* lay on the managers of the
" mission to show cause for continuing the
" experiment in that locality. I did not
" understand them to give any opinion as to
" the working of the mission in other places.
" It is conceivable that a plan which succeeds
" ill in some places may work well in others

* This passage is italicised according to the above copy,
as furnished by the Rev. George Webster.

" that are differently circumstanced. But
" they had in view the district which was
" under their own eyes, and which was com-
" mitted to their charge. And in that they
" (fairly, I think) called for proof of some
" good results. ' Lo, these three years I
" ' come seeking fruit on this tree and find
" ' none; cut it down.' If Dr. West had
" thought that both his present curates (as
" well as his late curate, Mr. Webster) were
" in error on this point, the next step would
" naturally have been to replace them by
" *others*. For it would manifestly have been
" unwise and hurtful to have two *independent*
" agencies going on in the same district
" without co-operation or mutual confidence.
" But as he did not think (nor did I) that
" there was any reason to think their dis-
" approbation was groundless, his only course
" was to request the suspension of the mis-
" sion in that locality. We *may*, perhaps,—
" both he and I, and the curates,—have acted
" on an error of judgment. But even if it
" were so, we ought not to be thereupon
" judged hostile to Protestantism. Nor,
" again, should any one assume as indubit-

" able that we must have erred in judgment
" because we differ from him on a question of
" *expediency*, not as to the *end* to be aimed
" at, but as to the *means* to be employed.
" For this would be to claim an infallibility
" beyond what the Pope pretends to. If my
" decision was an erroneous one, it was at
" least (as you know) not a *hasty* one. And
" this is more than can be said for those
" (and some such there are) who without
" having heard anything but an *ex parte*
" statement—and that (as I happen to know)
" a garbled and incorrect one—presume to
" pass severe censure on the archdeacon and
" me. I have ascertained that some reports
" are circulated by persons professedly friends
" to your mission, which are likely in the
" end to do more damage than any devices
" of opponents. For falsehoods, though ap-
" parently serving a present purpose, are
" sooner or later detected, and they do
" damage not only to the authors of the
" calumny, but also sometimes to the cause
" they advocate. It is reported, I find, that
" Dr. West concealed from me a letter from
" Mr. Eade (while I was in England) which

" would have caused my decision to be the
" opposite to what it was. This calumny is
" one which *would* have been worthy of the
" father of lies himself, except that it is so
" *silly* and *clumsy* a fabrication. For as I
" had all along determined (as you know) to
" examine the parties orally face to face, Dr.
" West *could* not, if he had wished it, have
" kept me in the dark on any point. The
" *truth* is that he did transmit to me the
" *whole substance* of Mr. Eade's letter, keep-
" ing the letter only as a memorandum for
" his interview with Mr. Eade previous to
" the oral examination before myself, which
" had been already resolved on. So that
" those who give credit to such a story as I
" have alluded to show great simplicity—I
" mean simplicity of *head*. But no honest
" man who knows anything of Dr. West
" would ever suspect him of anything dis-
" honourable, even when there is (as in this
" case there was not) some object to be
" gained by it. Those of an opposite cha-
" racter naturally suspect all men of being
" as unscrupulous as themselves. Some
" there are, 1 find, who profess to feel much

" esteem and veneration for me, only they
" lament my being in bad hands. I am a
" mere puppet, it seems, acting just as my
" evil counsellors pull the strings. This is
" just the manifesto of most rebels. They
" honour their king, and only rise in arms to
" drive away his evil counsellors. But I
" know how to value the esteem of such men.
" A little boy, indeed, may be on the whole
" a promising child, though he may have
" been seduced and bullied into something
" wrong by some naughty seniors; but a
" man of my age and in my station who
" should suffer himself to be misled by weak
" or wicked advisers would be clearly *good*
" *for nothing*. And such, therefore, must be
" the opinion those persons really have of
" me. I have mentioned as a specimen one
" out of many false reports that are circulated.
" If you should have it in your power in any
" degree to check them, you will so far be
" lessening a great danger both to your
" mission in particular and to the Protestant
" cause. For nothing could give a greater
" triumph to our opponents than to be able
" to point to persons professing to propagate

" the Gospel *truths* and yet setting the
" example of disregarding the *ninth* com-
" mandment even in their dealings with their
" fellow Protestants. . . . . Believe me, &c.,
" RICHARD DUBLIN."*

" I have in my possession an account,"
continues the Rev. George Webster, " written
" to me in October, 1857, of the investigation
" by one of the clergymen who were present.
" From this account it may be necessary to
" make some extracts, from which it will be
" plainly seen—(1) my letter to the Arch-
" bishop was not irrelevant to the subject.

---

* During Dr. Whately's reign in Ireland, he was constantly opposed in his Church policy by successive Deans
of St. Patrick's. These dignitaries owed their election
to the Chapter—a body which, until thinned by death,
proved true to the principles of Archbishop Magee.
The last Dean died within a week or two of Dr.
Whately, and was succeeded by Dr. West, his domestic
chaplain and confidential friend. One of the new Dean's
first public acts was to refuse the pulpit of Christ Church
for the sermons heretofore preached in support of the
Irish Church Missions. Evangelical wrath ran high at
this change, and hesitated not to assert that " Archbishop
" Whately packed the Chapter, with a view to the pro-
" pagandism of his opinions."—ED.

" (2) It will be seen his Grace condemned
" the giving bread to the Roman Catholics to
" make them attend the classes. (3) It
" will be seen how necessary it was for me
" not to subject myself to an action at law by
" publishing *names*, when *Mr. Eade declined*,
" *in the only privileged correspondence we had*,
" *to demand them from me;* for in his letter,
" December 30, he wrote, ' I am willing *to*
" ' *leave it to your judgment* as to whether
" ' they should be brought forward.' (4) It
" will also be seen when an honest, straight-
" forward parishioner was summoned by the
" Archbishop to testify what he saw with his
" own eyes, Mr. Dallas (the representative of
" a society with 30,000*l.* a year) warned this
" witness that his testimony (a testimony to
" be given for the sake of the Church of
" Christ) might be the subject of an action at
" law. (5) It will also be seen that this
" witness, when he was allowed to speak,
" made charges, *all of which were nearly the*
" *same as happened to be in my letter to the*
" *Archbishop.* The following extracts from
" an account of the trial may have some
" interest :—

"*Wednesday, Oct.* 21, 1857.

" In the front room were the Archbishop,
" the Archdeacon, Messrs. Dallas, ——,
" ——, ——, and ——, the witnesses, M——
" and S—— amongst them in the back-
" ground. Proceedings commenced with your
" letter being read. Then Mr. Dallas began
" to blame you for not mentioning ——'s
" conduct to him, and informing him of it.
" (That is of the conduct of one ordained
" agent who paid money to a person for
" acting the part of a Roman Catholic in
" the controversial class in Irishtown.) *The*
" *Archbishop said* —— (the ordained agent)
" *had been brought before him;* and Mr. Fitz-
" gerald (the Incumbent of Donnybrook) re-
" marked, he supposed you considered you
" had done your duty by informing your
" Diocesan. Mr. Dallas wanted to prove
" himself under his Grace yet intermediately
" to be consulted. . . . .

" Then came M—— (a most respectable
" parishioner of Donnybrook). Mr. Dallas
" cautioned him, as an action for libel might
" be the result of some of his statements ! ! !
" This nearly stopped the whole thing. Arch-

" bishop said, if anything said there was to
" be used, and not considered privileged, he
" would hear no more, and Archdeacon said
" he would then take steps as parish minister
" in the matter. Mr. Fitzgerald would not
" allow M—— to speak before Mr. Dallas
" promised all should be privileged. Mr.
" Fitzgerald made the charges, and now
" called M—— for evidence of them. Almost
" all M——'s evidence referred to ——'s
" time (the time of the ordained agent be-
" fore alluded to). The charges were read
" and their replies by the Archdeacon.
" M—— proved seeing F—— to have re-
" ceived money from —— (the ordained
" agent), and seeing his name in all the
" meetings, and men like him in all, he in-
" ferred they were all paid. They denied
" paying or ever knowing —— to pay. .
" . . . After much firing from them,
" and the charges and replies being read
" from sheets by the Archdeacon like briefs,
" W—— and Mr. Dallas holding the like in
" their hands, they offered no fruit of their
" noise and uproar, nor were they at all dis-
" comfited at none of their neighbourhood

" going (to the controversial classes). . They
" would have glorious fruit, Mr. Dallas said.
" His Grace asked for the blossoms. . . .
" I cannot remember all M——'s charges ;
" they were, however, nearly the same as
" your letter. What happened two years
" ago they disclaimed all knowledge of, and
" offered no apology. M‘C—— at one part
" gave the account of the man in their
" offices as to ——'s (the ordained agent's)
" giving —— money. This man, it seems,
" said you did not then (when you called
" at the office) charge —— with paying
" ——. I replied both at the time of ——'s
" doing so, you told me he had confessed
" it, and you on the evening of the day
" you had been in their office told me
" you had there told me of ——'s confessing
" it ; whereas their clerk told M‘C—— you
" had merely spoken of his hesitating and
" not liking to answer your question. . .
" . . On last Sunday Dr. —— passed by
" (Irishtown schoolhouse), and saw them
" giving bread, just such a scene occurring
" as you described. . . . . We had a
" private conversation with his Grace, who
" thought if the Irish clergy might vote by bal-

" lot, there would be a good majority against " them (*i. e.* against *the Irish Church Missions*), " but —— said any one now opposing would " surely be badly reported of. After his " Grace went, —— and —— spoke well of " M——. If it were a case of murder, no " evidence could be more straightforward."

It will be seen from the following specific charges that the Chancellor of Cork, who imbibed his views from Dr. Whately's lips, is utterly at variance with the leaders of the Irish Church Missions :—

" 1. That food and clothes are given to " poor Roman Catholics in Ireland by *the* " *Irish Church Missions Society*, to induce " these Roman Catholics to do what they " believe to be sinful.

" 2. That several years ago I made charges " against the society precisely the same as " the charges repeated in my correspondence " with Mr. Eade, and that these charges were " well known to the society, and especially to " Mr. Dallas himself and to Mr. Eade.

" 3. That these charges were made by me " against the society at an inquiry held by the " late Archbishop of Dublin, into the opera- " tions of the society in Donnybrook parish.

" 4. That after this investigation the Arch-
" bishop gave a judgment condemnatory of
" the society's operations in that locality."*

" I am willing to attribute to them the best
" of motives for their zeal in working *the*
" *Irish Church Missions*," proceeds Dr. Webster, " but I am firmly persuaded the offering
" of temporal rewards for violating conscience
" is regarded with displeasure by God, even
" though He may mercifully make many
" allowances for zeal that is not according to
" knowledge."

To renegade priests of the Roman Catholic
Church Dr. Whately gave no encouragement,
and we believe that in the entire diocese of
Dublin, Glendalagh, and Kildare, there is not
one officiating as a Protestant clergyman.

---

* " It is always reported in England," adds Dr.
Webster, " by the society, that not one shilling of the
" funds of *the society* is given for temporal relief in
" Ireland, and yet several thousands of pounds are raised
" in Ireland to provide food and clothes and lodging for
" the *converts* (?), with the full sanction of the society
" itself. This fund for temporal relief is part of
" the accredited machinery of the society, and to the
" present hour the temporal relief is given upon the
" expressed conditions that the recipients attend the con-
" troversial classes."

The Rev. Mr. C——, a Roman Catholic priest, who in unbridled pique at the arm of chastisement which his Bishop raised over him, opened a Presbyterian conventicle, and would have become a Protestant but that he repudiated all authority in matters of religion, was warmly condemned by Dr. Whately, especially for the virus with which, during the Famine, he contrived that one of the days on which the starving Catholics were to get soup should be Friday. Dr. Whately had probably this rebellious priest in his mind when he said, " Many a man re-
" nounces the shackles of Papal infallibility,
" as it were in a spirit of rivalry, that he may
" become a Pope to himself."

The men of genius who from being Roman Catholics became ministers of the Irish Church Establishment are few and famous; amongst whom Dean Kirwan and the Rev. Wm. Phelan may be regarded as, perhaps, the most prominent. But by far the greater bulk of those who sought office under Drs. Magee and Whately were thorough weeds from the Pope's garden, the value of which no one estimated more accurately than our

Archbishop himself. One individual called at the Palace whose mind, at no period very bright, was of late more than ordinarily clouded by the fumes of alcoholic stimulants. Dr. Whately, after a few questions, found that he was quite unfit for the sacerdotal office in any Church; and then, in accordance with a suggestion from his visitor, proceeded to examine him with a view to discharging the duties of a tutor. He broke down in Greek and Latin; but, as a last resort, declared to the Archbishop that he was well up in mathematics. "He has caught me " here," mused Dr. Whately, to quote his own words in telling the anecdote long afterwards; "for if there is one branch in my " ubiquitous smattering, of which, more than " another, I am less versed it is mathe- " matics.* However, I brushed up a suffici- " ently vivid remembrance of the Elements of

---

* Dr. Whately gave no attention to mathematics, as " it had no connection with human affairs, and affords no " exercise of *judgment*, having no *degrees* of probability." Another eminent logician, Sir William Hamilton, has denounced mathematics as the most illogical of sciences, and mathematicians as persons labouring under the worst species of infatuation.—ED.

" Euclid to ask him, with an air of considerable
" confidence, to describe a triangle. My
" visitor wrapped himself in thought for a few
" minutes, and then replied, that he would
" not undertake to describe a triangle verbally,
" but that if I could furnish him with pen,
" ink, and paper, he would be happy to draw
" one for my edification. I pushed him over
" the materials; after due deliberation he
" produced—

" instead of describing it solid, thus—

" The fact is, my visitor, who was a perfect
" clodhopper, knew no more of a triangle
" than the scales under that name which
" farmers erect in the fields for weighing
" potatoes ! "

Dr. Whately preserved for several years, as
a literary curiosity, the drawing by which
this rare candidate for holy orders and

academic duty desired that his proficiency might be gauged.

" Yours is a very queer bishop," remarked another convert, as he came down the palace stairs, after an interview with Dr. Whately. " I expected that he would have examined " me on transubstantiation and the Papal " supremacy; but, instead of that, he merely " examined me in Greek and Latin." The latter remark was addressed to the private secretary of Dr. Whately.

He would sometimes test in amusing ways the sincerity of convert aspirants to office in his diocese. " The diocese of Dublin, " Glendalagh, and Kildare," he once said, " is wide, but there are fields for the exercise " of pastoral activity still wider; and just " by way of trying your vocation, will you " oblige me by going on the mission, in the " first instance, for two years to New Zea- " land ? "

Dr. Whately endeavoured in some degree to compensate for his frigid impassiveness*

---

* A few years before Dr. Whately's death, some members of his family exhibited a desire to promote

towards the Irish Church Missions and the Evangelical Alliance, which had mainly for its object the " propagation of the Gospel," by taking the chair and making a speech at the meetings of the Dublin Auxiliary of the South American and Patagonian Mission.

" I believe," he said, " the society is pro-
" ceeding in the wisest and most rational
" manner, by making civilization and religion
" go hand in hand. I believe the savage, so
" long as he continues a savage, is incapable
" of being a Christian. The characteristic
" of savages is improvidence. The man who
" can be hardly brought to think of to-
" morrow, much less to sow his land in the
" hope of reaping a harvest in five or six
" months afterwards, will listen with great
" apathy when spoken to about the next
" world. They should see the example of
" civilized men provident in the things of
" this world, and be taught the common
" arts of life. Then they will be brought to

Proselytism by ragged schools, and other agencies, but the Archbishop himself not only took no part in the project, but, as we have heard, deprecated it.

" see that those persons have their interests
" and welfare at heart, and gradually learn
" the advantages of providence and fore-
" thought. You will find the result will be
" that they will be brought to place their de-
" pendence and faith at last not on the things
" which are seen and temporal, but on the
" things which are not seen and are eternal.
" That is the way we train children. What
" would be the use of telling a child of two
" or three years old what is to happen in
" after life or after death ? He can be only
" brought to comprehend some immediate
" benefit or advantage. As he grows older,
" he will come to think of some reward to be
" given him three months hence, at the end
" of a school or college term. By degrees we
" are led on, by little and little, to place our
" faith in that which is more remote, and,
" of course, if we proceed like real rational
" human beings, we will be 'enabled, by
" divine grace, to place our hopes, anxieties,
" and cares, not on the things of this world,
" but the next. That is the way we must
" proceed with savages, who are, in fact,
" adult children. They must be taught to

" place faith in what is more and more
" remote—First, in that which will take
" place in six months or a year; and then
" they will be brought at last to think of
" the care of their eternal souls. Let no
" one, therefore, disparage this society for
" proceeding slowly, by teaching, first, the
" rudiments of civilization and arts of life,
" and laying, by that means, the founda-
" tion on which to build the superstructure
" of future knowledge."

The scantiness of attendance in some of
the Protestant churches of Ireland has been
the subject of serious comment and brighter
joke since the days of Swift. The latter, in
satirical allusion to a certain church wherein
the congregation was almost literally limited
to the parish clerk, remarked that the
preacher should have interlarded his homily,
not with "Dearly beloved brethren," but
"Dearly beloved Rogers." The witty canon
of St. Paul's, Sydney Smith, has described
" the well-paid Protestant clergyman, preach-
" ing to stools and hassocks, and crying in
" the wilderness."

We once heard a good story told, descriptive of a parish in a remote part of Ireland, where the parson and priest lived on terms of great intimacy, owing doubtless to the fact that the parson had not the ghost of a congregation, and was therefore exempt from that bitterness to which opposition or rivalry often gives birth. "My dear fellow," said the latter, "I have a favour to ask. " My bishop is coming down here next week " on his first visitation, and it is absolutely " necessary that I should make a respectable " appearance. I want you to lend me your " congregation for an hour or two, and you " have my word of honour that no religious " rite shall be performed." The priest, who was a humorist as well as a goodnatured man, is said to have entered into the joke, and consented, provided that no divine service should be gone through in presence of his flock. The bargain was struck; the bishop came down; the congregation was marshalled before him; and the parson was unctuously complimented, and, as the story goes, rewarded by preferment, for the highly creditable state of religion in his parish.

These and other kindred imputations Dr.

Whately would seem to have clubbed together in his mind, preparatory to disturbing them with one of his amusing retorts. "Those," he said, "who are continually calling attention "to the empty or half-empty churches in "some parishes, while wholly overlooking "the three times as many parishes in which "there is a distressing want of church ac- "commodation, seem to proceed in the way "that Balak did with Balaam, 'Come now "'and I will bring thee to another place, "'where thou shalt see but the uttermost "'part of them and *shalt not see them* all; "'and curse me them from thence.'"

CHAPTER VII.

THIS contest between Dr. Whately and the Roman Catholic party, on the question of National Education, did much to redeem, in the estimation of *his* flock, "the errors of "liberality" into which his earlier life had been betrayed, and a lull in the storm which had so long pursued him succeeded; but after a time it was again lustily revived.

During the lull to which we refer, the old Archbishop, at a civic banquet in Dublin, could not help congratulating himself on the "signs of the times." We well remember his hand quivering with palsy, as he spoke the following :—" I have long since been for- "given an offence which, perhaps, was at first "considered a grievous one—that of being "an Englishman; but I think you have learned "by experience—not only in my case, but in

" very many others—that it is possible for
" those born elsewhere to be the true and
" zealous friends of Ireland. Since I came
" amongst you I have never changed. I have
" never encouraged—on the contrary, I have
" always desired to repress—that narrow,
" paltry, provincial spirit that would separate
" island from island, county from county, one
" portion of the British Empire from another.
" I have never regarded Ireland as a province
" —as a dependency of England. I have
" never ranked her as a subordinate or de-
" pendent country, but have always regarded
" her as an integral part of the great British
" Empire; and you may be assured he is no
" friend either to Great Britain or to Ireland
" who would seek to sow the seeds of rivalry
" and hostility still between the two coun-
" tries; and I would further say that I extend
" that sentiment not only to Ireland but to
" every part of the British Empire in every
" part of the world. In my own time it has
" happened that two very eminent prelates
" who have been raised by their great merits
" to the bench of bishops of England, were
" natives of—not of Great Britain—but the

" little paltry island of Barbadoes. Suppose
" the feeling had been nourished of Barba-
" does for the Barbadians, would these pre-
" lates ever have attained their high dignity?
" Why if we were to carry out the narrow
" sentiment of Scotland for the Scotch, Ire-
" land for the Irish, we would have Dublin
" for the Dubliners, Cork for the Corkonians,
" which would, in many respects, be very in-
" convenient." Dr. Whately, in his ecclesiastical policy, advocated the same view.

The prelates to whom Dr. Whately alluded
were Dr. Samuel Hinds, his first private
secretary, and appointed in 1849 Bishop of
Norwich, with an income of £4,465 a year;
and Dr. Renn Dickson Hampden, his contemporary and friend at Oxford. (See p. 86,
ante.)

An eminent thinker has pointed out the
danger of allowing a dominant thought to
assume a proportion to the rest of the faculties which was not in proportion with its own
value. " Never allow," remarks Cardinal
Wiseman, who in his recent lecture on Self-
culture has let us into the secret of his own
intellectual system—" Never allow what might

" be considered a favourite idea, or fancy, or
" imagining, to dwell for any length of time
" in the mind. It had been said, and he be-
" lieved with truth, that there was hardly a
" mind so strong as not to have within it the
" possible seed of insanity, and that seed
" might be found in this form—a single idea,
" without any reason to account for its taking
" possession of the mind, might go on de-
" veloping until it became a sort of morbid
" feeling, resulting in the manner which he
" had indicated."

Dr. Whately ran the danger, but did " not
" perish therein." Many years ago he became an enthusiastic believer in mesmerism.
Its various ramifications under the names of
od-force, biology, and animal magnetism, he
embraced with equal devotion. He often
spent whole days in concentrating the analytic
powers of his mind upon the consideration of
their bearings. He was delighted with the
idea, and could speak or dream of nothing
else. He went from one extreme to another,
until he avowed an implicit belief in clairvoyance, induced a lady who professed it to
become an inmate of his house ; and some of

the last acts of his life were excited attempts at table-turning, and enthusiastic elicitations of spirit-rapping. He never was so happy as when eliciting outbursts of this sort. Instead of laying spirits, like the prelates of old, he boasted of being able, like Yorick, " to set " the table in a roar."

On mentioning to a friend some extraordinary circumstance connected with clairvoyance, he expressed incredulity.

" But you have the evidence before you," replied the Archbishop.

" But the evidence may be deceived," said his companion ; " and I frankly avow that I " am a complete sceptic of everything con- " nected with clairvoyance."

" Do you presume to limit the power of the " Almighty ? "

" No ; but does your Grace go so far as to " assert that a miracle has been performed ?"

" No miracle at all," he went on to say ; " only the operation of a natural law."

His companion was posed.

" Remember," he added, as usual following up his advantage, " that Harvey, who dis- " covered the circulation of the blood, was

" ridiculed by his fellow physicians, and
" called ' Circulator,' which is the Latin for
" quack ; and both astronomy and electricity
" were copiously ridiculed in their time, not
" only by the author of ' Hudibras,' in a satire
" on the Royal Society, soon after its estab-
" lishment, but by many others."

Dr. Whately was of opinion that an error
in physics and science is nothing so long as
it is not taught as a part of religion. " If
" taught as such, it becomes a lever placed
" underneath a man's religious principles,
" which will heave up and overthrow them ;
" for as soon as he discovers it to *be* error,
" he thinks he has got a demonstration of the
" falsity of the revelation, of which he has
" been told it is a part."

We wish we could feel sure that the Archbishop's credulity in these wonderful experiments was never abused by designing con-
federacy. He seems to have had at no time
any suspicion that the many operators before
whose experiments he stood ecstatically en-
chained, exaggerated the effect of those experiments by the aid of accomplices. In all
other inquiries Dr. Whately was impregnably

on his guard against delusion ; in those now
under consideration he surrendered his faith
implicitly. To even the truths recorded in
Holy Writ he applied his inexorable logic.
Take, for example, the following :—" It is
" worth while to remark that, in all the cases
" recorded of angels bringing messages from
" heaven, a sufficient test was provided to
" secure the persons concerned from being
" misled by any delusions of imagination,
" and to assure them sufficiently of its being
" a real communication from heaven that
" they had received. The finding of a babe
" lying in the manger at the inn, as the shep-
" herds had been told by the angel, saying,
" ' This shall be the sign unto you,' proved
" clearly that they had not been dreaming,
" or deluded by any fancy. Again, the
" absence of the body of Jesus from the
" sepulchre, and afterwards his own appear-
" ance to the disciples, attested the truth of
" the announcement of his resurrection. And
" again, the actual release of the Apostles
" from prison was of course a proof perfectly
" decisive that there was no delusion. And,
" as Dr. Paley has justly remarked, either

" Cornelius's vision, or Peter's—taking each
" separately—might, conceivably, have been
" a delusion : taking the two conjointly and
" connected, as they were, with each other,
" there could be no doubt of the reality of
" either."

Mrs. Whately was, as we have said, a
person of considerable attainments, elegance,
and worth. She and her husband had many
views in common ; but without that perpetual interchange of mawkish acquiescence
which often imparts insipidity to social life.

" Two people," truly remarked the Archbishop, "who are each of an unyielding
" temper, will not act well together ; and
" people who are *all of them* of a very yield-
" ing temper, will be likely to resolve on
" nothing ; just as stones without mortar
" make a loose wall, and mortar alone no
" wall. So says the proverb—

> " 'Hard upon hard makes a bad stone wall,
> But soft upon soft makes none at all.' "

Partly executed by Mrs. Whately and
partly by her husband, who pruned her
redundancies in the same spirit with which

he strengthened his trees,—by lopping—some
little books of a moral aim appeared ånony-
mously in 1830.

With this gifted woman Dr. Whately lived
and loved for eight-and-thirty years ere any
domestic bereavement saddened their hearth.
Then, for the first time, the hand of death
began to be heavily laid upon the family.
A favourite daughter, just married, was
stricken down; and immediately afterwards
another domestic bereavement, though not
the work of death, followed. " Ten years it
" has added to my age," the Archbishop
said.

On Mrs. Whately these afflictions told still
more fatally.   She died 25th April, 1860.
" He was one of the most tender-hearted
" fathers," observes the Rev. Maurice Neligan, " and anything more solemn or more
" affecting was never witnessed than his
" conduct at the time of the death of his
" dear wife; he sat down upon the stairs
" outside the chamber, and wept like a child
" while the sad change was approaching.*

---

* A lengthy dissertation has recently been published
by a physician of France on the beneficial influence of

" He was most tender and affectionate in all
" his family relationships, and never was
" happier than when, round his own fireside,
" he was shedding the light of his own bril-
" liant and profound criticism over the pages
" of some well-known volume. In private
" he was full of sympathy, tenderness, and
" gentleness."

It will be admitted that the strong natural
feeling noticed by Mr. Neligan was more
ennobling in the outburst than ever it could
have proved in the suppression. It was a

groaning and crying on the nervous system. He con-
tends that groaning and crying are the two grand
operations by which nature allays anguish—that he
has uniformly observed that those patients who give
way to their natural feelings more speedily recover
from accidents and griefs than those who pronounce
it unworthy of manhood to betray such symptoms of
cowardice as either to groan or cry. He is always
pleased by the crying and violent roaring of a patient
during the time he is undergoing a trying surgical
operation, because he is satisfied that he will thereby
soothe his nervous system so as to prevent fever, and
insure a favourable termination. He relates the case
of a man who, by crying and bawling, reduced his
pulse from one hundred and twenty-six to sixty in the
course of two hours.

momentary ebullition of feeling, irresistible
and uncontrollable; but once over, a murmur
never after dropped from his well-disciplined
breast.

Archdeacon Wolseley says:—" Deeply tried
" in the furnace of affliction by successive
" domestic bereavements of those most dear
" to him, I never heard him utter, nor heard
" of his uttering, a word of complaint or of
" murmur."

The Chancellor of Christ Church, Dr.
Tisdall, writes : — " While those bereave-
" ments were lying heavily at his heart, and
" his health was becoming visibly impaired,
" the duties of his office were discharged with
" zeal and assiduity, and it was not until the
" fatal arrest was laid upon his physical
" energies that he ceased from exertion."

The Archbishop was an advocate for early
marriages, and so anti-Malthusian in his
views that a strong expression of Polygamical
Theology was drawn from him, under curious
circumstances, within a few months of the
very period to which we have just referred.
In connection with the South African Mission,
to which, unlike the Irish Church Missions,

the Archbishop had given the authority of his name and sanction, it was represented by the clergyman charged with the duty of reporting progress, that an influential native chief had expressed a willingness to embrace Protestantism provided that he should not be required to discard some half-dozen wives to whom he was ardently attached. The missionaries, who held out to the pluralist not much hope of a dispensation, regarded with poignant regret what seemed a serious hitch in the progress of their mission; but as a last resource they wrote to Dr. Whately for advice as to the best course to pursue in the dilemma. We remember to have read at the time the Archbishop's reply, which is not now within our reach; but the substance was to receive the polygamist chief by all means, and that he should not be required to discard the several women of his choice.

How Dr. Whately could have applied his logic satisfactorily to this decision is curious. St. Paul, in whose writings he was profoundly versed, invariably speaks of marriage in terms implying the union of one man with one wife. Dr. Whately once said that not only are many instances of polygamy recorded in the Scriptures, but it is nowhere distinctly forbidden. Unhappily, however, for the Archbishop's generous views on the subject of conjugal society, it is very explicitly written that " a " *bishop* should be the husband of *one* wife." But even from this passage an inference favourable to polygamy as regards the laity is drawn by Milton in a posthumous work strongly advocating polygamy, which, edited by the chaplain of George the Fourth, was published some five-and-thirty years ago.

The expulsion of Dr. Whately's books from the National Schools, and the general droop of that once powerful system of education, were owing quite as much to Protestant as to Catholic influences. The defeat of his favourite scheme by allied influences, generally unsociable, was a thought which, during the remainder of Dr. Whately's life, never failed to give a barbed stab to his heart. He was a man to whom the word "fail" had been, from his earliest youth, unknown; and in his decrepitude he was obliged to fold to his breast the humiliating consciousness of failure. The thought would cling to him like the old

man of the mountain, and he would try to
cast it off with such struggles of his muscular
logic as, " He only is exempt from failures
" who makes no efforts." In his last Charge,
delivered on 16th of June, 1863, the old man
cast one longing, lingering look behind at the
edifice he had anxiously planned and lovingly
raised, but which he had now in disgust and
despair forsaken. " Of all the wonders (and
" they are not few or small) which have ap-
" peared in the last half-century, this will
" probably be accounted by our posterity as
" the most marvellous. They will regard it
" as a thing above all others strange and
" unaccountable, that when an opening was
" afforded for imparting to Roman Catholics
" as well as to Protestants—under the sanc-
" tion of Roman Catholic ministers, a large
" amount of Scriptural instruction — an
" amount which probably would have led
" many of them, in after-years, to the study
" of the entire Bible,—this work should have
" been strenuously and perseveringly opposed,
" and finally defeated by Protestants."

In this Charge Dr. Whately took a fling at
Bishop Colenso, though not with the warmth

of his brother "Manchester," who denounced him of Natal as a person who had assailed the Pentateuch "by misrepresentation the " most unpardonable, by distortions of the " truth the most monstrous, and with a ' " savage glee and exultation which would " rather become a successful fiend.

" Mankind," said Dr. Whately, " may often " be found to vibrate, as it were, from the " extreme to the opposite. We may take as " an instance of the misapplication of a just " principle, the injudicious advocacy which is " now prevalent of the doctrine of toleration. " It is a doctrine perfectly right in itself; *i.e.*, " no one ought to be liable to secular penalties " for conscientious religious error; but this " doctrine may be, and has been of late, so " misapplied as to justify the conduct of one " who retains office in a Church (be it a sound " or an erroneous Church) to whose doctrines " he is opposed."

At the Dublin Meeting of the British Association in August, 1857, there was no more active member than Dr. Whately, whether as President of the section, or king of the conversazione. He refuted the assertion that economic science was hostile to charity, and added that it was misdirected charity only to which exception could be taken.

Failing health and bitter domestic affliction prevented the Archbishop from being present in 1861 at the meeting in Dublin of the National Association for the Promotion of Social Science, "and we thought," writes Dr. Hancock, "that increasing infirmities " would prevent his taking further part in our " proceedings;* but last session he came to " our opening meeting to hear the address of " the Solicitor-General.† Later in the ses- " sion he contributed a paper containing the " notes of a conversation between himself and " Mr. Senior on Secondary Punishment, and " took part in the discussion which followed— " thus devoting his latest energies to promote " that reform in punishments which he had " been so instrumental in producing, and " selecting our society as the means of con- " veying his views to the public."

His appearances in public were now few

* The Dublin Statistical Society.
† Mr. Lawson, late Whately Professor of Political Economy in the University of Dublin.

and far between; but in the retirement of his study his mind continued to seek a wide range of popular influence. Until a short period before his death several recently started serial publications received no stint of his contributions. To beginners —in the walk of magazine progress—he was ready to lend a helping hand; as soon as they seemed able to get on without him, he withdrew his friendly aid. To Dr. Norman M'Leod's publication, *Good Words*, Dr. Whately contributed, until 1862, a series of papers entitled "Passages from my Note-"Book," which are of a critical and suggestive character, and show that his mind retained its old sympathies and sparkle. During former years he had been a large contributor to the *Saturday Magazine* and also to the *London Review*, which, however, is not to be confounded with a more recent publication under the same name.

Like the waters of a lake, generally calm and pellucid, but occasionally roused into formidable activity, the intellect of Whately, clear to the end, was sometimes rippled by side-winds, and would rise into vigorous waves which lashed angrily around. As an illustration, his last Charge, delivered in June, 1863, may be consulted.

One of his last retorts conveyed a telling stroke of delicate irony. " They will begin " to pelt me now," said a freshly fledged Bishop, who sought consolation under the weight of a mitre laden with some suspicion of a temporizing compliance on the Education question.

" They have nearly given over that prac- " tice upon me," observed the Archbishop.

" Well, no. one can say that I ever threw " a stone at you," retorted the other.

" Certainly not," was the reply; " you " only kept the clothes of those who did."

So far as paying his subscription regularly, Dr. Whately was a member of the Royal Irish Academy ; but he took little or no part in its labours or deliberations. On visiting its Museum, shortly after his. arrival in Ireland, he viewed with suspicion and hearty incredulity almost every Celtic relic, and confidently pronounced them to be of obviously Roman origin. These views he subsequently much modified, especially when his attention had been directed to the very beautiful gold articles in which the Museum is so rich. He latterly consented to fill the honorary office of Vice-President, and in this capacity used sometimes to saunter into the Academy during an evening meeting, attended by three or four of his favourite chaplains; but he always took up position in a room different from that in which the meeting was being holden, and started an opposition entertainment in the shape of a conversazione, if such it could be called, when the Archbishop talked the whole time himself, and we are bound to add, talked well. This marvellous flow of talk began about seven, and generally lasted until after eleven o'clock. Notwithstanding his occasional presence in this shape, Dr. Whately was accused of an indifference to Hiberno-Celtic literature, and to the archæological proceedings of Ireland, which made him unpopular with Irish archivists and antiquarians, who compared his alleged desire of Anglicising Ireland to the efforts of the Romans to blot out all other languages but their own. Viewing Ireland as an integral

part of the great British empire, he rather
deprecated all distinctive badges of nation-
ality, which he invariably stigmatized as a
" paltry provincialism," calculated to separate
island from island.*

To Irish literature of more general interest, Dr. Whately was equally indifferent,
feeling that he knew quite as much on the
subject as he cared to know; and it more than
once happened, that Irish authors who sent
" Presentation Copies" to the Palace, were
never thanked. "The Macaria Excidium"—
a work quoted by Macaulay in his History—
was presented to Dr. Whately by the author;
but no notice was ever taken of the gift; and
we heard the same complaint made by the
late Dr. Fulton.

The Statistical and Social Inquiry Society
of Ireland was more to his taste, and indeed

* When engaged one evening in a disquisition on the
difference between the Irish and Scotch Celts, Dr.
Whately gave a pleasant fillip to the conversation when
it threatened to become dry, by suddenly asking, by the
way, " What is the difference between an Irishman and
" a Scotchman on the top of a mountain in frosty
" weather?"—" One is *cowld* with the kilt, and the other
" *kilt* with the *cowld !* "

it may be said that he was the parent as well as the President of it. He rode on his richly caparisoned hobby of political economy to inaugurate it; and this valuable science is the basis of the Statistical Society. The Archbishop at one of its meetings rather happily observed that—

" Without casting any disparagement upon " the other societies which existed in Dublin, " such as the Zoological Society, and the " Natural History Society, of which he him- " self was a member, he thought that in " comparison with those, this society might " be addressed in the words of Virgil :—

" Excudent alii spirantia mollius æra,
　Credo equidem, et vivos ducent de marmore vultus;
　Tu regere imperio populos, Romane, memento;
　Hæ tibi erunt artes." ·

" For the world must be governed, has been " governed, and will be governed by political " economists, though many of them were " very bad ones."

The great progress which the Statistical Society has made in its labours, and the steadily increasing accession of workers at its Council and Board, prove that the Society was not started before it was needed.

Of the Royal Dublin Society Dr. Whately never became a member. He had been intending to join it until the black-beaning of Archbishop Murray by that body provoked an opposite resolution. He remarked to a friend that " were he to be elected after Dr. " Murray's rejection, it might widen the " wound of which that fatal step was " productive."* For this respected prelate

---

* Perhaps the only Roman Catholic who remained calm under the wound was Dr. Murray himself. With much dignity we find him thus acknowledging the tender of an *amende* which some influential members contemplated :—

" MY DEAR CORBALLIS,—

" It is to me a subject of unaffected concern, that I " have become most unintentionally a source of disagree- " ment amongst the members of the Royal Dublin " Society. It has been my object through life to conciliate, " not to disunite ; and it could not, of course, fail to be " peculiarly distressing to my feelings to be an occasion " of dissension in a body, which, if united, is so well " calculated to do extensive good, and the combined " efforts of all whose members are so much wanted for " the improvement of the country. As far as I am con- " cerned, all future discussion on the subject of the late " ballot would be entirely useless. The decision come to " on that occasion was final. It has disclosed the fact " that my co-operation for the advancement of the purhe entertained a cordial friendship; and he felt the slight with something of personal pique. Another circumstance occurred which helped to promote the latter feeling. Dr. Whately, shortly after his arrival in Ireland, consented to take the chair at an evening meeting of the Royal Dublin Society; but a majority of the body pronounced ineligible for that position any person not a member.

Dr. Whately gave kindly help to the Industrial Exhibition at Cork, in 1852; but his aid was given guardedly. " This National " Exhibition," he said, " has not been got up, " as far as I can observe and collect, from " any spirit of rivalry or jealousy against the " Great Exhibition in London last year, but " it has been got up in a spirit of honest and " laudable emulation ; not to show how well " Ireland can get on without England and " the rest of the world, but to show how " worthy Ireland is to be included in the in- " dustrious nations of the world, and how " worthy it is to form a portion of the British

" poses of the Society would not, in the opinion of a con- " siderable portion of its members, be likely to prove " beneficial."

" empire. And as there has been no feeling
" of jealousy exhibited in getting up this Ex-
" hibition, so I hope no feeling of low narrow-
" mindedness or base jealousy will be excited
" in England against it. If the English should
" see as much to be admired as I have seen
" this day, I conceive the natural effect will
" be congratulation to the Irish, and increased
" emulation amongst the English. I think I
" may say that the National Exhibition, if
" not more admirable than the Great Exhi-
" bition, may be called more surprising, con-
" sidering the circumstances under which
" each was got up."

Dr. Whately also extended his patronage
to the " Central Young Men's Christian Asso-
" ciation," and delivered on its platform an
original and argumentative lecture on the
Jews. The Archbishop draws an ingenious
parallel between the Zingaries or Gipsies and
the Israelites, whose idiosyncrasy he carefully
analyzes.

To the Historical or Debating Society of
Dublin University Dr. Whately showed no
favour, or, when brought under his cutting
criticism, gave no quarter.

The Historical Society, during its first era, is an exciting tradition in Ireland; it was the great nursery of Irish eloquence and patriotism, and its sons numbered, amongst others, Plunket, Bushe, Tone, Moore, Miller, Parsons, the Emmets, and Burrowes. Such an institution had no tendency to anglicise Ireland; and the Archbishop condemned it. But it is due to him to say that other reasons influenced this view.

" The young person who, by the exercise " of debating societies, is hurried into a " habit of fluent elocution—of ready extem- " poraneous speaking, which consists in " *thinking* extempore —will be found to have " been qualifying himself only for ' the lion's " ' part,' in the interlude of Pyramus and " Thisbe. ' *Snug.*—Have you the lion's part " ' written ? Pray you, if it be, give it me ; " ' for I am slow of study.' *Quine.*—' You " ' may do it *extempore ;* for it is nothing but " ' roaring.'

" To those engaged in debating societies," he went on to say, "the temptation is very " strong to transgress the rule, which every " speaker ought to observe, of never allowing

" himself, in one of these mock debates, to
" maintain anything that he himself believes
" to be untrue, or to use an argument which
" he perceives to be fallacious; because, to
" such persons as usually form the majority
" in one of those societies,—youths of imma-
" ture judgment, superficial, and half-edu-
" cated,— specious falsehood and sophistry
" will often appear superior to truth and
" sound reasoning, and will call forth louder
" plaudits; and the wrong side of a question
" will often afford room for such a captivating
" show of ingenuity, as to be to them more
" easily maintained than the right. And
" scruples of conscience, relative to veracity
" and fairness, are not unlikely to be silenced
" by the consideration that, after all, it is no
" real battle, but a tournament; there being
" no real and important measure to be actually
" decided on, but only a debate carried on for
" practice sake."

A few years before his death, Dr. Whately
appointed to a responsible office connected
with a society in which he took considerable
interest, a gentleman who was already known
to hold another and a higher office elsewhere.

A violent attack upon the Archbishop appeared in a leading Irish journal, accusing him of stupidity, and pronouncing as a self-evident proposition that one of the first acts of his nominee would be to betray the trust, and sacrifice the last appointment to the interests of the office previously held. "That " is the suggestion of a corrupt mind," said Dr. Whately, taking off his glasses and throwing the paper to a friend ;—" the man who " imputes such motives would be the very " first, if placed in a similar situation, to " betray us, and degrade himself."

Partial paralysis of the left side had now set in, and Dr. Whately became extremely feeble; but, true to early instincts, he was ready to die in harness. " Not satisfied with " speaking to us from his study," writes one of his flock, " we sorrowfully remember " him coming round to see us in his confir- " mations; and in the performance we see " this aged prelate so exhausted that he has " been forced to sit down to recover strength " to place his trembling hands upon our " expectant heads."

Until disabled by the final stroke, the

Archbishop was to be daily seen in Stephen's Green, drinking fresh air, and seeking strength. Sometimes he would work his arms round and round like a windmill; at other times he threw pebbles at birds, or romped with his exuberant dogs.

It is remarked by the biographer of Bishop Jebb, that the prelate's mind during the closing years of his life would often seek repose; but, like the pendulum of a clock, it only needed the slightest touch to set the machinery in active motion.

Whately's mind, as we have said, frequently bounded, and even wounded by its strokes; but after a storm comes a calm, and a reaction often succeeded those bounds. Othello's occupation, however, was not wholly gone. Touch him with a genial allusion or a pleasant poke, and "RICHARD was "himself again."

Leaning on the arm of his chaplain, the Archbishop was met at this time by an old friend whose powers of pedestrianism had been often envied. "I hope your Grace is "very much better to-day," said the friend. "Oh, I am very well, indeed, if I could only

" persuade some strong fellow like you to
" lend me a pair of legs," was the reply.

" I shall be only too happy to give you
" *my* legs if your Grace has no objection to
" give me *your* head in exchange."

The Archbishop brightened up at the
touch of wit and delicately conveyed compliment—he was always peculiarly ignitable
by both—and, laughing heartily, exclaimed,
" What, Mr. ——, you don't mean to say
" that you are willing to exchange two *under-*
" *standings* for one." One retort led to
another, until it was a complete game of bat-
tledore and shuttlecock between them.

Touching the word " either," he was asked
whether *E-ther* or *I-ther* was the correct pro-
nunciation. " *Ni-ther*," replied his Grace.

Had Dr. Whately nursed his leg, it would
have been better for him. He would seem to
have given too literal an interpretation to a
theory of Dr. Thomas Whately, a kinsman of
his, who in 1799 published " The Cure of
" Ulcers on the Legs *without rest*."

The attack of senile gangrene which, in
July, 1863, disabled Dr. Whately's leg, might
possibly have been arrested in its course by

active remedies ; but Dr. Whately refused to swallow any medicine, and more than once conveyed to his advisers the view " that " they might throw physic to his dogs, who, " however, although they dealt in *bark*, were " better judges than to drink it." This insuperable repugnance to medicine was partly the result of a charlatanical course of drastic drugging to which the Archbishop, shortly after his arrival in Ireland, was sub-jected, and partly because homœopathy was a medical paradox, and on principle he liked all paradoxes. The attempted cure proved, in his case, much more fatal than the dis-ease which it aimed to remove; and ever after Dr. Whately limited his faith in medicine exclusively to the homœopathic system. He went further, and henceforth withdrew all aid from the medical charities of Dublin, of which he had been previously a generous supporter.

Meanwhile his views of death were clear and vigilant: " Admirable as is the whole " of God's creation, no other of His works " can be so interesting to man, as man him-" self; sublime as is the idea of the eternal " Creator Himself, our *own* eternal existence

" after death is an idea calculated to strike
" us with still more overpowering emotions.
" That man, feeble and short-lived as he
" appears on earth, is destined by his Maker
" to live for ever — that ages hence, when
" we and our remotest posterity shall have
" been long forgotten on earth—and count-
" less ages yet beyond, when this earth itself,
" and perhaps a long succession of other
" worlds, shall have come to an end — we
" shall still be living; still sensible of plea-
" sure or pain, to a greater degree than our
" present nature admits of, and still having
" no shorter space of existence before us
" than at first — these are thoughts which
" overwhelm the imagination the more, the
" longer it dwells upon them. The under-
" standing cannot adequately embrace the
" truths it is compelled to acknowledge; and
" when, after intently gazing for some time
" on this vast prospect, we turn aside to
" contemplate the various courses of earthly
" events and transactions, which seem like
" rivulets trickling into the boundless ocean
" of eternity, we are struck with the sense of
" the infinite insignificance of all the objects

" around us that have a reference to our pre-
" sent state alone."

As regards resurrection of the *body*, he held,
somewhat peculiarly, that " this hope depends
" not on the resurrection of the very same
" particles of matter,—an idea which has
" needlessly exposed it to cavils from infidels
" to which neither reason nor revelation afford
" means of replying. For, as during this life
" all the particles of a man's body are under-
" going a perpetual and rapid change, that
" which constitutes it his body is not the
" identity of the materials, but their union
" with the same soul, and performance of
" similar functions. And that there should
" be such a change in the raised body, is no
" more inconsistent with the promise made
" to the Christians, than it would be if a
" kind benefactor, who had engaged to rebuild
" for a poor man his house that had been
" destroyed, employed in the erection other
" and different materials ; it would suffice that
" he had, as before, a house ; and one that was
" suitable for all the same purposes."

Of a more wholesome animus are his
thoughts on death.

" When men talk of preparing for death," he said, " they mean preparing for the next life."

" Many a one trusts to the mercy of God, " who has never thought seriously of the " conditions of that mercy."

" Though it may never be too late to repent, " it is always too late to think of deferring " repentance."

" Of his last illness and closing days on " earth you will not expect me to speak " fully," observes the Rev. H. H. Dickinson. " I could not trust myself to do it, nor should " I like to do what his own truly unboastful " spirit and genuine humility would most have " shrunk from—repeat last words and say- " ings meant for a few. His whole religious " life and conversation were thoroughly " genuine and natural. That was their " charm and freshness; and they were " natural and consistent, and even charac- " teristic, up to the last."

Dr. Whately had often contemplated with a shudder the cruel penalties which had laid their grasp upon the once vigorous intellect of his predecessor, Dr. Magee. Can we doubt that this terrifying example was in his

mind when he made the remarks to which
his chaplain, the Rev. H. Dickinson, thus
refers:—"All through his life it was his
" prayer—and often he had asked the prayers
" of others also—that God would leave him
" his reason to the last, or, as he expressed
" it, 'would let him live no longer than
" ' he should be alive.' His prayer was
" answered. His faculties remained unim-
" paired. Under the lowest extreme of bodily
" prostration, he was himself in intellect and
" mind up to the end."

We have heard another chaplain say, that
one reason of the horror with which Dr.
Whately regarded an imbecility of mind was,
lest he should be induced in hours of mental
weakness to administer the duties of his
office in a way from which in the full vigour
of his intellect he would have recoiled.

"Bishops," said the Rev. Sydney Smith,
" in the decay of strength and understanding,
" will be governed, as all other men are, by
" daughters and wives. Hence I have known
" wife bishops and daughter bishops."

We do not say that Dr. Whately antici-
pated any undue interference on the part of

his own family. But various persons had, at different times, sought, generally with un-success, to maintain an ascendancy over him.

The Rev. Dr. Salmon's impressions of the closing scene are equally interesting :—

" We had not known all his claims on our
" affectionate regard until his tedious and
" painful illness revealed many a gentler
" grace, for the display of which there had
" been no opportunity before. He had not
" only to endure severe and long-continued
" pain ; he had to submit to what was even a
" harder trial than pain, when a mind of no
" ordinary activity, retaining all its energy,
" found the body unable to respond to its
" wishes, and then he was reduced to a state
" of utter helplessness peculiarly trying to
" one of unusual independence of spirit.
" Under this trial his friends found him con-
" stantly full of thoughtful considerateness
" for others, present and absent, most grateful
" in acknowledgment of services rendered,
" supported by a strong sense of Christian
" duty, which survived his bodily decay,
" and with pitying admiration they saw all
" his force of character exerted to battle
" down every inclination to murmur, and to

" control any expression of petulance or im-
" patience which could add to the sorrow of
" those who ministered to him. I own I
" take more pleasure in recalling these things
" now than in speaking of the more public
" and more prosperous part of his life."

The dreadful torment which filled every
moment of his last long month on earth,
could probably have been alleviated by the
judicious administration of anodynes and
opiates; but Dr. Whately, like Fox and
O'Connell, refused to swallow drugs.

The Archbishop used to say with Voltaire
that we ought not " to thrust drugs of which
" we know little, into a body of which we
" know less."

His friends, notwithstanding, persistently
urged him to take medicine; but he replied
in the words of another thinker, that their
advice was like their physic, more pleasant
to give than to take.

He could lay aside the joke, however, and
qualify his hostility to physic when the
bodily ills of a friend seemed to claim medical
intervention. One of the last letters which
we have seen from the Archbishop is addressed to a favourite chaplain whom he had

inoculated with the whole of his peculiar views. Long-continued ill health had sapped this clergyman's constitution; but, true in fidelity to the dogmas of his chief, he would not consult a physician nor swallow a remedy. He considered that medicine would only add fuel to the flame. The Archbishop's letter to him is eminently affectionate and characteristic. He beseeches him to lose no time in consulting a physician, and, lest the clergyman should still hesitate, he urges the additional persuasive of " *canonical obedience.*" The appeal was, we believe, unsuccessful.

In many graver instances Dr. Whately found it difficult to remove impressions which he had himself sometimes half in joke made.

On Monday, September 14th, it seemed that a few hours more would terminate his sufferings. Surrounded by his family, he partook on that* day, and for the last time, from the hands of Bishop Fitzgerald and Archdeacon West, the Sacrament of the Church of England. The natural vigour of his constitution, however, offered a more de-termined battle to the approach of death, than either physician or friends thought possible.

" No rebellious murmur," says Dr. Dickinson, " escaped the lips that in long nights of
" mortal pain prayed constantly for patience."
" A few days before his death," remarks the
Rev. Maurice Neligan, " one of his clergy
" said to him, ' Well, your Grace, it is a great
" ' mercy that, though your body is weak, your
" ' intellect is vigorous still.' ' Talk to me no
" ' more about intellect,' he replied ; ' there is
" ' nothing for me now but Christ.' "*

* Dr. Whately when at Oxford preached strongly on
" Preparation for Death ; " and this able lecture was one
of his last republications.

" We have, indeed," he says, " no right, and God
" knows we have no wish, to set bounds to the Divine
" mercy, and to pronounce that a dying repentance even
" of the most hardened sinner is certainly unavailing.
" And we should say that for the dying man the death-
" bed is the best time for seeking to make his peace with
" God, simply because he has no other. For any one
" else, we should say that it is the very worst, because
" such repentance is the only kind whose sincerity cannot
" be proved to himself or to others by yielding fruits, and
" because it is the only kind to which Scripture makes
" no promises, and to which, consequently, we have
" no right to make any. We warn you that the
" time to prepare for the Lord's coming is now, and
" at every time when you least expect it, and we are
" ready to teach you how that preparation should be
" conducted."

The Archbishop's death was slow and ex-
cruciating; but a troop of faithful friends
surrounded him, and it was not their fault if
they failed to smooth the dying prelate's pillow.
He would have no nurse but them. The Vicar
of St. Ann's says, " No one but He who doth
" not willingly afflict could tell the sufferings
" which were an agony to see."

Another of his chaplains, the Rev. Robert
Dickinson, refers to the touching scene of
which he was an eye-witness, and tells us that
" the dying prelate seemed more solicitous
" about the pain he was giving others than the
" suffering he was enduring himself."

The bulletins issued during the last two
days of Dr. Whately's life were to the effect
that " His Grace was sinking rapidly." On
Wednesday, October 7th, he lost the power
of speech ; but the mind struggled to the last
against its threatened dethronement. A few
minutes before noon on the following day all was
over. Dr. Whately having died in the country,
his remains were removed to the Palace, where
they lay for some days in state, whilst church
bells round tolled with muffled peals.

The funeral was a public one, and included,

among other attending bodies, the clergy of Dublin and Kildare, the provost, fellows, professors, and scholars of Trinity College, Dublin, with its representatives in parliament, the senate of the Queen's University, and the Royal Irish Academy with its mace. His Excellency the Lord Lieutenant, the Lord Chancellor of Ireland, the Lord Mayor, the Dean of St. Patrick's, who survived Dr. Whately by some weeks only, and F. M. Lord Gough, were also present. The mourning coaches, which were eight in number, contained, with others, the Rev. E. Whately; George Whately, Esq.; Rev. W. L. Pope, brother-in-law of the deceased; the Bishop of Killaloe; Archdeacon West; Archdeacon O'Regan; Archdeacon Wolseley; the Rev. H. H. Dickinson; M. Kevork Ohanessian, of Constantinople, whom the deceased had adopted, and the deceased's medical advisers. The carriages of the nobility and gentry helped to swell the procession, which was met at the western door of Christ Church by the chapters of the two cathedrals. The remains were then conveyed to the chancel, while the fine funeral service of Handel and Morley, performed by full choir, swept through the same grey old walls wherein High Mass had whilom been intoned. Among other Roman Catholics in the *cortége* were Chief Justice Monahan, Mr. Justice Keogh, John Ennis, Esq., M.P., J. R. Corballis, Q.C., P. P. MacSwiney, Esq., Lord Mayor elect, and Alderman Moylan, D.L.

He used to say, with the Roman, that all his dignities came upon him before he wished for them, and left him before they were desired by others. It is to be hoped that a report, seriously calculated to disturb the latter portion of this gratifying thought, failed to reach the dying prelate, and embitter by its stab the last struggle in his battle of life.

"The public," says the *Mail*, "will be "loth to believe that, while Archbishop "Whately was expiring, a Court of Claims "was sitting upon the competing pretensions "of rival churchmen, and that his high office "was actually given away while he was "living. A great and unusual scandal like "this would not tend to reconcile the Church "and the public to otherwise odious appoint- "ments." The writer then proceeds to mention a rumoured series of promotions which, he added, " would be received with the pro- " foundest disquietude by the Church and " the Protestant people of Ireland."

It is probably not the fault of the candi- dates that these rumoured appointments were not made.

A scramble for a mitre, by the ejaculators of " Nolo Episcopari ! " even before the eyes beneath that mitre were closed in death, is, we fear, no novelty; and from the days of Primate Boulter, more than one instance might be cited of such unseemly struggles almost behind the bed-curtains of the dying man. On March 4th, 1724, Boulter, wri- ting to the Duke of Newcastle, says, that there have been "repeated advices from " England, that upon the report of the Arch- " bishop of Dublin's illness, there was a very " great canvass on the bench about his suc- " cessor, without the least regard to what " might be· represented from hence, as of " service to his Majesty."

Dr. King balked for a time the premature calculations of the expectant bishops. Two years later Boulter writes with ill-disguised

satisfaction to say, that Dr. King " *has*
" *of late been pretty much out of order;* "
and on February 9th, 1726, he descants " in
" relation to the filling up of the Archbishop-
" ric of Dublin whenever it happens to be
" vacant." We may remark, that the policy
suggested by Boulter has been almost invariably acted upon. " I am entirely of opinion
" that the new Archbishop ought to be an
" Englishman, either already on the bench
" here, or in England : as for a native of
" this country, I can hardly doubt but what-
" ever his behaviour has been, or his promises
" may be, when he is once in that station he
" will put himself at the head of the Irish
" interest in the Church at least ; and he will
" naturally carry with him the college and
" most of the clergy here." *

---

* Boulter kept a close eye on the health of the
bishops. In a letter to the Duke of Newcastle, dated
Dublin, September 11, 1725, he says :—

" MY LORD,—
" As I had the honour of writing to your Grace by
" the last post, I should not so soon have given you a
" new trouble, but for an accident that has since hap-
" pened to the Archbishop of Cashel. Whilst his lady
" was bathing his leg with brandy or spirits, they un-

George Browne, the first Archbishop of Dublin after the Reformation,* was an Englishman; and the same remark applies to his immediate successors, Hugh Curwen and Thomas Jones. Dr. Margetson, who succeeded in 1660, was a native of Yorkshire, Francis Marsh (1681), of Gloucestershire, and Narcissus Marsh, of Wiltshire. William King, for whose removal to a happier and a better world Primate Boulter expressed strong anxiety, was a native of Antrim, and as a vigorous thinker and energetic worker, occupies no minor niche in the gallery of illus-

―――――

" fortunately took fire, and his leg is so hurt by it that " his life is thought to be in great danger. As his post " is the third in this Church, and has a good income be- " longing to it, I thought it my duty to give your Grace " immediate notice of the danger he is in." The "leg," we may add, recovered.

* Dr. Whately, by the way, considered the epithet " Reformation" infelicitous, and calculated to injure rather than serve the Protestant interest. " The " Restoration," he once remarked to his chaplain, " would have been a much more effective name." But he did not think the " Restoration," as designating the accession of Charles after the Cromwellian interregnum, expressive. It ought to have been called " The " Relapse!"

trious and distinguished Irishmen.* Dr.
King was succeeded by John Hoadley, an
Englishman, and brother to the learned
Bishop of Winchester. Dr. Hoadley, resign-
ing in 1742, Dr. Charles Cobbe, a native of
Winchester, assumed the see of Dublin. The
Hon. Wm. Carmichael, son of Lord Hynd-
ford, Archdeacon of Bucks, and some time
Bishop of Meath, was consecrated Archbishop

---

* Dr. King's ablest lucubration was the " Origin of
" Evil," a subject to which Dr. Whately also turned his
thought and pen; and according to some critics both
might have been better occupied.

" The question," writes Whately, " concerning the
" Origin of Evil is left by the Scriptures just where they
" found it. They neither introduce the difficulty, as
" some weak opponents contend, nor account for it, as is
" imagined by some not less weak advocates, who, having
" undertaken to explain it, and having, perhaps, satisfied
" themselves and others that they have done so, are sure
" to be met by the very same difficulty reappearing in
" some different form; like a resistless stream, which
" when one of its channels is dammed up, immediately
" forces its way through another. He who professes to
" account for the existence of evil by tracing it up to the
" *first* evil recorded as occurring, would have no reason
" to deride the absurdity of an atheist who should profess
" to account for the origin of the human race, by simply
" tracing them up to the first pair."

of Dublin in 1765 ; but dying a few months later, Dr. Arthur Smyth became his successor. John Cradock, a native of Wolverham, and a graduate of Cambridge, assumed the archiepiscopal mitre in 1772. In 1778 Dr. Cradock gave place, according to the natural course of events, to Dr. Fowler, previously Prebendary of Westminster, who was succeeded in the arch-see by Dr. Charles Agar, an Irishman, created in 1806 Earl of Normanton.

Dr. Euseby Cleaver, a native of Buckinghamshire, and brother to the Bishop of St. Asaph, was consecrated Archbishop of Dublin in 1809. Until his promotion to the Primacy in 1822, Lord George Beresford was—for the term of two years—Dr. Cleaver's successor, but his life is more legitimately connected with the Church history of Armagh. Dr. William Magee, to whom we have already so frequently made reference, was the first Irishman of mark—with the exception of Dr. King—who since the Reformation filled the see of Dublin.

On the promulgation of the report that at the suggestion of the highest person

T 2

in the realm the see had been offered to Canon Stanley by Lord Palmerston, a very energetic outcry was raised in Dublin against his appointment.

" The action," exclaims one sentinel, " ought to be instantaneous and decisive. " What was done in England when Magee " was nominated to a bishopric there ?—a " man who honoured the Bible as the word " of God. What was done in England when " the late Lord Plunket was nominated " to the Rolls there ? Let us not deserve " the contempt of posterity, but stand to a " manly assertion of our rights.

" The insult," screams a second, " termin-" ates in the King of Kings, whose authority " is ignored by the appointment of one who " rejects his miraculous agency."

" Should Dr. Stanley be forced on us," observes another, " I trust that the arch-" bishop and bishops will refuse, one and all, " to consecrate him; and if all unite in a " protest, they may defy the efforts of any " government to corrupt the doctrines taught " by the Church of Ireland—an effort which " in this instance seeks to do so by giving us

" a man who does not believe honestly in the
" miracles in the Word of God."

Meanwhile, an influential newspaper announced the appointment as absolutely
made; and the ruffled flock were urged to
be resigned to a visitation more painfully
trying than the phrase Episcopal Visitation
generally bears. " No ! " exclaims an uncompromising Calvinist, " it would be a
" downright mockery of religion. I am
" sure that there is not a Protestant clergy-
" man or layman in Ireland who will not, if
" it comes to the worst, sign a petition to
" the Crown against the appointment of this
" Neologian, and not only that, but contri-
" bute to any expenses.

" We would like to know the best and the
" worst of our new archbishop," writes a
Churchman half resigned to a fate which
now seemed inevitable, " but alas ! we
" cannot tell whether the glitter and brilliancy
" of his style may be the clear gleam of
" the water of life or the deceitful mirage of
" the desert."

Another clergyman, appreciating the apophthegm that the better part of valour is

discretion, recommended that Dr. Stanley
" be met in a fair and liberal spirit, as other-
" wise he may throw himself into a clique;
" and we have seen enough of that already.
" It is more than probable that the author of
" Arnold's life will boldly and manfully ex-
" press his opinions; and, blessed be God,
" we have good scholars, not alone in Greek
" and Hebrew, but in the Bible, the essence
" of all true learning, when he gives a fair
" opening, to meet him fairly and openly,
" and we may look for the Almighty's bless-
" ing as to the results.*

* This terrible storm would seem to have been entirely
evoked by the following note, printed at p. 521 of Dr.
Stanley's " Lectures on the Jewish Church." He begins
by saying " that his lectures having been in substance
" written before his tour to the East, they are 'irrespec-
" 'tive of any of the works which have been recently
" 'published on the Criticism and History of the Old
" 'Testament,' but that 'it is due to the interest excited
" 'by one of the works to which he alludes, to state in a
" 'few words its bearing on the present volume.'"

He then proceeds to say, obviously alluding to the
volume of Bishop Colenso, that—

" The arithmetical errors which have been pointed out
" (with greater force and in greater detail than hereto-
" fore, but not for the first time, by eminent divines and

On Monday, October 26, a meeting of the Protestant clergy of Dublin was held at 16, Upper Sackville-street, nominally for the " purpose of united prayer, that the mind of " our Government, in selecting a successor " to the late Archbishop of Dublin, might be " directed to the appointment of one every " way qualified," but in reality to protest against the appointment of Canon Stanley.

Whether the prayers or the protest, or neither, worked their end, we shall not pause to discuss.

The announcement that Dr. Stanley was not to be Archbishop after all, and that the see had been virtually accepted by the Very Rev. R. Chenevix Trench, D.D., Dean of Westminster, took all Ireland, including even the petitioners and protesters, by surprise. The storm ceased; and in the words of the sacred volume with which it was sought to knock down Canon Stanley, "there was a great calm."

" scholars) in the narrative of the Old Testament are
" unquestionably inconsistent with the popular hypothesis
" of the uniform and undeviating accuracy of the Biblical
" history, or with the ascription of the whole Pentateuch
" to a contemporaneous author."

The scion of a Galway family, though by
birth and education an Englishman, the
owner of a considerable property in Ireland,
the great-grandson of Richard Chenevix,
Bishop of Waterford*—the husband of an

* Among the monuments in the old church of St.
Mary, Dublin, is one containing the following inscription :—

" Near this place lieth the Body of

" MRS. CHENEVIX,

" Daughter of the late Col. Dives, of Bedfordshire,

" and Wife to the Right Rev. Richard, Lord

" Bishop of Waterford and Lismore,

" A Lady formed by Divine Providence for the Residence
" of all Christian Virtues and every amiable Quality.
" To her superior understanding, Improved by a generous
" Education and much reading, were joined a Benevolent
" and Obliging Disposition, and an affable and courteous
" deportment, which, with a peculiar liveliness of Spirit
" and Wit, rendered her conversation entertaining and
" instructive, and qualified her to sustain the different
" Stations of life in which she appeared with high repu-
" tation. She abounded with the truest signs of a
" most affectionate tenderness towards her husband and
" Children, of kindness to her Relations, of Charity to
" the Poor, and faithfulness to her friends. In return
" for these Excellencies she was loved and esteemed by
" all that knew her, particularly by her Royal Mistress,
" the Princess of Orange, and her friend the Countess of
" Chesterfield. Her last sickness, which was long and
" severe, she bore with all the patience and fortitude

Irishwoman—connected with the Whites of Woodlands, the Marquis of Drogheda, and other Irish families, the appointment of Dr. Trench was regarded by the Protestants of Dublin (who had long been accustomed to the dominion of strangers by blood, birth, and feeling) as a step in the right direction, albeit that their new Archbishop had been the intimate colleague of the High Church Bishop of Oxford—whose brothers have become Roman Catholics—and was known to share largely the views of his chief. In the matter and manner of their preaching, it is difficult to distinguish any difference.

Dr. Trench's appointment to the see of Gloucester, in 1855, was prematurely announced; some hitch occurred, and the

" which Reason and Religion could give, and continued
" intent on her Devotions till, with her last breath, on
" the 30th day of June, 1752, she recommended her
" Soul into the hands of her Almighty Creator and Most
" Merciful Redeemer.
    " To her Memory, which will be ever honoured by and
" dear to him,
    " This Monument was erected by her Most Affectionate
" Husband."

bishopric was given to Dr. Charles Baring, the nephew of Lord Ashburton. Archbishop Trench was born in September, 1807, and is therefore in his fifty-seventh year. This is not the place to enumerate the many substantial evidences of his literary taste and talent which give him a high position among the men of the time.*

The province of Dublin, of which he is

---

* While Dr. Whately steered his course clear of the errors of his predecessor, Dr. Magee, Dr. Trench has already shown a substantial disposition to avoid the mistakes into which Dr. Whately fell. When the latter first arrived in Ireland, he seemed to view the clergy superciliously, and he gave mortal offence by sending to England for his brother to preach the consecration sermon. Of this mistake Dr. Trench has kept widely clear.

The Rev. Dr. Lee was in his rooms in Trinity College, Dublin, when a gentleman entered, who, in a quiet and modest way, said, "I presume, sir, you are "the Rev. Dr. Lee?" The other bowed. "I wish," rejoined the stranger, "you to preach my consecration "sermon, and to confer the favour on me of becoming "my chaplain." Then, and for the first time, Dr. Lee saw before him the Archbishop-designate. They were total strangers to each other personally, but Dr. Trench had known and liked Dr. Lee through his writings. Dr. Lee is popular with the clergy of his Church; and the selection was in good taste as well as good policy.

head, embraces the suffragan dioceses of
Ossory, Ferns and Leighlin, Limerick, Ard-
fert and Aghadoe, Cork, Cloyne and Ross,
Cashel, Waterford, and Emly, and Killaloe,
Kilfenora, Clonfert, and Kilmacduagh. The
archdiocese itself includes the counties of
Dublin, Kildare, and Wicklow, with portions
of Wexford, Queen's county, and King's
county. The annual income attached to
the archbishopric is £8,000.

CHAPTER VIII. AND LAST.

ONE of the organs of Irish Protestantism, in announcing the death of Dr. Whately, and the rumoured appointment of a successor, said, " It is sometimes easier to paint a per- " fect bishop than to find a respectable one."* Those who hold that biography should read like the inscription on a mural monument, may consider that in our volume Archbishop Whately's shades of character have been too freely touched; but the nineteenth century is pretty generally of opinion that the maxim of the first, " *De mortuis nil nisi bonum*," may be followed too literally, and that the substi- tution of " verum " for " bonum " would be more in accordance with the growing intel- ligence of the age. Mr. Catterson Smith's

---

* *Dublin Evening Mail*, Oct. 9, 1863.

celebrated portrait of Dr. Whately would never have been pronounced "a speaking " likeness," had the artist omitted those touches of shade which so effectively relieve the brighter portions, or cloaked that extra-ordinarily-shaped head, which, although em-bracing thought as clear as rock-water, was, phrenologically considered, unintellectual in its formation. But the idiosyncrasy of Dr. Whately involved inconsistencies much more curious as a study. With a reputation for being the ablest logician of the day, and an examinator of evidence searching and un-sparing, he believed implicitly in od-force, clairvoyance, spirit-rapping, mesmerism, and homœopathy. To this catalogue might be added "phrenology;" but he propounded his notions on the system much more charily than as regards the others—apparently alive to the delicacy and awkwardness of avowing himself a phrenologer in the face of his own peculiarly-shaped head. His adhesion to these upstart sciences is the more remarkable when we hear, on the authority of a writer in " The New Review," that " he despised " philosophy, and poured contempt on meta-

" physics." Evidential and rationalistic in his own tendencies, he yet castigated Rationalists in his last Charge. A rigid economist in theory, he scattered every farthing of his immense official income; but this was an inconsistency of which to be proud. Eminently an original thinker, and an inculcator of originality of thought and expression, he condemned extempore prayer, and assigned their indulgence in it as one of his reasons for discountenancing the Evangelical Alliance. But then, on another occasion, he met an objection to prayer on the ground that it was unnecessary, because God must know our wants, whether we supplicate him or not, and aptly replied: " True ; He knows our wants, " but not our humble supplications to Him for " aid, unless we make such supplications. " Now, it is to our prayers, not to our wants, " that His gifts are promised. He does " not say, ' *Need*, and ye shall have ; *want*, " ' and ye shall find ;' but, ' *Ask*, and ye shall " ' have ; *seek*, and ye shall find.' "

With great masculine sense, he was childlike in his simplicity, and before, his arm became palsied, might be seen on Sandymount

Strand, like a schoolboy on the playground, throwing a boomerang. Of this toy he was excessively fond; and during the dull intervals of a visitation, he would frequently beguile the tedium by cutting miniature boomerangs from card, and shooting them from his finger. But he had other and older " Diversions of Purley." He would throw a " stick or roll a turnip," observes an Oxford reminiscence, " for the amusement of his " dogs in Christ Church meadow." He was simple in another way. " He was very un- " suspicious of dishonesty in others," remarks the Rev. H. Dickinson ; " and owing to this " cause was sometimes perhaps deceived."

An inculcator of the law of Christian politeness, and a stickler for the great principle, " Good manners are a part of good " morals," he yet often went out of his way to transgress both. Generously tolerant of the religious doubts of other creeds, and of a peculiarly sceptical tendency himself, he could not brook any difference of opinion expressed in depreciation of his own caprices. The consequence was that a chosen few constantly surrounded him, all ardent admirers of the magnificent monologue of which he was master, and ready to applaud him through every mood and tense. Thus, while professedly " broad " in his views, he enclosed himself within a narrow circle, round which the censer constantly swung to the apotheosis of the high priest of their adulation.*

* We make no allusion to some amiable and gifted men on whom Dr. Whately bestowed many marks of regard and reward; and from some of whom we have ourselves received evidences of kindly feeling. The parasites to whom we refer belonged to both genders. One party used to feign absence of manner, and would often blurt out—in the Archbishop's presence, as though unconsciously—" What a mighty genius ! How good ! " How great ! How marvellous ! " And we are assured that Dr. Whately, although quite aware of these utterances, always failed to see the servile spirit which prompted them. Dr. Whately had more than once recorded in print his admiration of unconscious manners.

" Though many conscious people," he writes, " are " very agreeable, there is a charm in unconscious " manners, which endears a person, even when there is " nothing else very remarkable in him. Social inter-" course is in itself a pleasure, independent of the " instruction or entertainment we may derive from the " matter and language ; else books would be—which they " are not—a complete substitute for society : hence it " appears, that the essence of social intercourse is the

But few men were less narrow-minded. In his " Lecture on the Influence of Profes- " sions on the Character," he says that " against this kind of danger the best pre- " servative, next to that of being thoroughly " aware of it, will be found in varied reading " and varied society, in habitual intercourse " with men, whether living or dead, whether " personally or in their works, of different " professions and walks of life, and, I may " add, of different countries and different " ages from our own."

Dr. Whately, in limiting his intercourse with men, compensated for that contraction by an immoderate communion with hetero- geneous literature; and was, therefore, when he mixed in society, peculiarly qualified to talk *de omnibus rebus*, &c.

" interchange of ideas, as they arise actually in the minds " of the speakers; the excellence of it, therefore, in " social intercourse, must consist in complete uncon- " sciousness; the further you recede from that (and " there are infinite degrees), however clever your con- " versation, the less have you of the nature of a " companion, and the more of a book; consequently " consciousness is, as it were, the specific poison of that " which is the very essence of conversation."

" His habit of rapid and diligent reading,"
writes one who knew him well, " combined
" with a remarkable tenacity of memory and
" an intense conviction of the impregnability
" of his own conclusions, caused his writings
" to reflect not only the light of other minds,
" but also his own special views, with a pe-
" culiar concentration, which, had they been
" less intrinsically liberal, might occasionally
" have seemed supercilious."

Of any interference in his episcopal conduct
Dr. Whately was very jealous; and although,
as he would say, certain friends had his ear,
he never allowed them to lead him by the
nose. Clear-sighted on most points, Dr.
Whately could never see through flattery, or
the obvious motives of adulatory acquiescence; and if his eye did sometimes pene-
trate the former, it is surely inconsistent that
a man who plumed himself on an uncompromising love of truth, should not reprobate
untruthful because indiscriminate praise.
Like doctors of another sort, who never swallow their own prescriptions, Dr. Whately too
often forgot the apophthegms which are propounded in his own books. In his Logic,
under the head of " Fallacies " (p. 175), he

says :—" The applause of one's own party is " a very unsafe ground for judging of the real " force of an argumentative work, and con- " sequently of its real utility. To satisfy " those who were doubting, and to convince " those who were opposed, are the only sure " tests ; but these persons are seldom very " loud in their applause, or very forward in " bearing their testimony." It is matter of notoriety that " ditto " rather than " where- " fore " was the general murmur heard round the archiepiscopal table, from the head of which the hospitable host dropped, to quote the impression of an admirer, " conversa- " tion indescribable—as finished as Macau- " lay's studied sentences—with a marvellous " power of impromptu quotation and illus- " tration, as ready, rich, and happy."

The ease with which Dr. Whately swallowed flattery startlingly contrasts with the repugnance which he often expressed towards it. An illustration not only of this anomaly, but of the Archbishop's fatal art of speaking brusquely, occurred at a lecture given, a few months ago, in Dublin, by Mr. A. K. H. Boyd, "On men of whom more might be

" made." Lord Carlisle, the popular Viceroy of Ireland, in language of peculiar grace, proposed a vote of thanks to the lecturer, which the Archbishop consented to second. " I shall " not express," said his Grace, " any opinion " of the lecture, for two reasons; first, be- " cause it is in extreme bad taste to praise a " man to his face; and secondly, if you be " not capable of forming an opinion of it " yourselves, nothing that I could say would " enable you to do so. I shall probably take " another opportunity of giving an opinion " which is at least valuable for its sincerity."

Dr. Whately, although generally fond of acquiescence, was, as we have seen, too sound a logician " to dislike a legitimate sub- " ject of logical discussion ; " and when he met his match, or one courageous enough to avow it, few were more ready to unfold greater strength of argument and wealth of illustration in support of some novel paradox.

But he denounced sophistry, and still more fallacies. " Sophistry," he said, " like poison, " is at once detected and nauseated, when " presented to us in a concentrated form ; " but a fallacy which, when stated barely in " a few sentences, would not deceive a child,

" may deceive half the world, if diluted in a
" quarto volume. It is true, in a course of
" argument, as in mechanics, that 'nothing
" ' is stronger than its weakest part,' and
" consequently a chain which has one faulty
" link will break ; but though the number of
" the sound links adds nothing to the *strength*
" of the chain, it adds much to the chance of
" the faulty one's *escaping observation.*"

And yet, although he powerfully reprobated
sophistry and fallacies, he could rarely speak
of Ireland without—probably unconsciously
—tinging his theme with both.*

Dr. Whately considered his mind searchingly exhaustive in its power of inquiry, yet,
according to a recent critic, " it was rather
" inclined to rest on general principles which
" required further analysis ; yet his deductive
" reasoning from such had every step in the
" process carefully secured against the intru-
" sion of paralogism or fallacy. He thus
" could conduct an argument with severity
" and acumen, though seldom, if ever, with
" subtlety."

* The Archbishop repeatedly declared—and, as all
Ireland knew, erroneously—that it was trades'-union
strikes which deprived the country of its commerce.

With " Be just and fear not " for his motto,
and intrepidly just in most actions of his life,
he was largely influenced by favouritism in his
appointments ; and his clergy complain that
" unshorn striplings rather than masters in
" Israel " received promotion at his hands.
But at the same time it must be admitted
that there never was a man so little tinged by
nepotism, or who exercised the patronage in
his gift with less consideration for selfish
instincts ; and it is much to the advantage of
this prelate's fame, that while five of his
chaplains have become bishops, it is only
within the last year that he presented his
son, Edward Whately—who has been fifteen
years in orders—to the comparatively poor
parish of St. Werburgh's.   With this excep-.
tion there is not, in the united dioceses of
Dublin, Glendalough, and Kildare, a single
officiating minister who is either connected
with, or related to, Archbishop Whately.
And here we cannot avoid contrasting him
once more with his predecessor, Archbishop
Magee, of whom his biographer declares that
" during his lifetime he provided munificently
" for his sons, four of whom he brought

"up in his own principles and profes-
"sion."*

Other anomalies besides those already
noticed marked Dr. Whately's character.
Full of philanthropy and constantly moved
by the most tender emotions of compassion
and affection, he had, as we have seen, a
fatal habit of dropping remarks and allusions
which sometimes seared their way into the
hearts of those around him. This is the more
remarkable when we know—what few have
hitherto known — that Dr. Whately was
himself painfully alive to snarls ! The Rev.
H. Hercules Dickinson, referring to the irre-
verent unpopularity which pursued him,
records :—

"I tried to act as if I did not feel it," were
his own words, "but it has shortened my

* "Memoirs of the Archbishops of Dublin," by John
D'Alton, Esq., M.R.I.A., p. 360—a work quoted with
praise by Dr. Whately in the Appendix (pp. 41–42) to
his Charge delivered in August, 1851. It is curious that
Mr. D'Alton in his "Memoirs of the Archbishops of
"Dublin," remarks (p. 360) that "all endeavours to
"obtain for his work any authentic or satisfactory par-
"ticulars of the life of Dr. Whately utterly failed."

" life."*   " Few beyond those who knew him
" best," adds the Vicar of St. Ann's, " could
" guess the pain it was to a nature which was
" as trustful as it was guileless, to be so much
" distrusted and misrepresented as he once
" was."

Dr. Whately has been styled, by a writer
in " Notes and Queries," " the Sydney Smith
" of the Irish capital." The style of their
wit, however, was by no means identical.
When the witty Canon of St. Paul's spoke
of a cannibal chief inviting an omnivorous
friend to partake of roast Rector and corned
Curate, it was rich humour ; when Whately
said to a clerical valetudinarian who consulted him on the propriety of going to New
Zealand for his health, " By all means go—
" you are so lean no Maori could eat you
" without loathing ; "—it was a telling stab.†

---

* It may be said that Dr. Whately, having attained
his 76th year, outstripped the average age. The
Whately family are proverbial for longevity. His
sister, Lady Barry, aged 84, still lives; and the same
remark applies to Thomas Whately, now entering on his
ninetieth year.

† On some few occasions the Archbishop got a Roland
for an Oliver. It was, we believe, the Hon. Dr. Le Poer

From the specimens we have given, it
will not excite wonder that of Dr. Whately's
conversation, impressions should strangely
differ. " His conversation, fascinating beyond
" expression," records one, " was adorned
" with graceful and sometimes startling com-
" parisons, warmed with genial humour, and
" made even more attractive by frequent
" flashes of keen and sparkling wit, while
" all was toned down by moderation and
" exquisite charity of thought." *

" He was addicted to jokes," exclaims
another, " in which the quality of the wit
" did not compensate for the sharpness of

Trench, last [Anglican] Archbishop of Tuam, who, in
casual conversation, slightly misquoted a classical passage. Dr. Whately having indicated the error rather
with the rough whirl of a teacher's birch than with the
gentle touch of an episcopal crosier, was interrupted with,
" My Lord, I cannot lay claim to much scholarship or
" erudition, but I must congratulate myself on not being
" of the number of those whom learning has made
" mad!"

To give the Archbishop his due, he took retorts of
this sort in good part; but they came few and far
between, and the records of their utterance will never
fill a " Joe Miller." The preponderance of the retorts
are all upon the other side.

* Saunders' News Letter, No. 37,955.

" the sneer they frequently carried." * But
in justice to his memory, it is right to bear
in mind that " he had no notion of the
" stinging vigour of his words, and often
" inflicted pain without the faintest idea that
" he had done so." †

He himself said that " to be always
" thinking about your manners, is not the
" way to make them good ; because the very
" perfection of manners is *not* to think about
" yourself." ‡ Thus it would appear that
his brusqueness was in a great degree the
result of a false discipline. ||

We are willing to believe that Dr. Whately's

* *Dublin Evening Mail*, No. 8,267.

† *Saturday Review*, No. 416.

‡ " Thoughts," p. 10.'

|| Since expressing this opinion, our view has been
corroborated by one of Dr. Whately's chaplains, who
writes :—" There was an occasional abrupt uncere-
" moniousness and inattention to superficial courteous-
" ness arising from absence of mind, or rather pre-
" occupation with something of importance, that natu-
" rally struck those who met the Archbishop only in
" casual society."

We have seen the following remark in one of Dr.
Whately's writings, which is not irrelevant :—

" It is remarkable that great affectation and great
" absence of it (unconsciousness) are at first sight very
" similar ;—they are both apt to produce singularity."

occasional proneness to say cutting things arose not from a desire to pain feelings worthy of respect, but was owing, in the first place, to his indomitable love of sincerity, and in the second, to the often involuntary practice of thinking aloud, which has characterized many men of great intellectual attainments, including Lord Dudley.* To

* Moore records several amusing anecdotes of Lord Dudley, based on his odd habit of making comments aloud. A gentleman who proposed to walk with him from the House of Commons to the Travellers' Club heard him mutter—" I think I may endure the fellow " for ten minutes." Lord Auckland used to tell a curious fashion Lord Dudley had of rehearsing over to himself, in an under tone, the good things he is about to retail to the company, so that the person who sits next to him had generally the advantage of his wit before any of the rest of the party. The other day having a number of the foreign ministers and their wives to dine with him, he was debating with himself whether he ought not to follow the continental fashion of leaving the room with the ladies after dinner. Having settled the matter, he muttered forth in his usual soliloquizing tone : " I think we must go out " all together." " Good God ! you don't say so," exclaimed Lady ———, who was sitting next him, and who is well known to be the most anxious and sensitive of the lady Whigs with respect to the continuance of the present Ministry in power. " Going " out all together " might well alarm her. On another

particularize more fully these awkwardnesses in this place would be to incur in our own person still more gravely the blame which was occasionally laid at the Archbishop's door.

But hard words break no bones, and it was of late years pretty generally admitted, even by the smitten, that Richard Whately, with all his faults, might be worse. Any person who has studied the writings of Whately must have been struck by occasionally stumbling on a twice-told tale or startling paradox, all the more startling from a shrewd suspicion that you had seen it once or twice before. These repetitions were not accidental but intentional. It was a special rule with him to recur to, and lay down, over and over again, certain principles which he held in esteem. He wisely considered that one stroke of the

occasion, when he gave somebody a seat in his carriage from some country house, he was overheard by his companion, after a fit of thought and silence, saying to himself, "Now; shall I ask this man to dine with me "when we arrive in town?" It is said that the fellow-traveller, not pretending to hear him, muttered out in the same sort of tone, "Now; if Lord Dudley should "ask me to dinner, shall I accept his invitation?"

hammer was not enough to drive home his wedges or holdfasts. In conducting an argument he was always astute—invariably keeping the conclusion.out of sight until he had formidably marshalled his proofs. In fund of illustration always apt, generally ingenious, but rarely picturesque, no author with whose works we are acquainted has approached him, and unless in the authorized version of the Bible, we do not think his style has been surpassed.

Dr. Whately wrote the purest English. In all his multifarious writings there is not one affected expression, and hardly one foreign word; and he even went so far as to keep clear of words of foreign extraction. " That style," he said, " which is composed " chiefly of the words of French origin, while " it is less intelligible to the lowest classes, " is characteristic of those who, in cultiva- " tion of taste, are below the highest. As " in dress, furniture, deportment, &c., so " also in language, the dread of vulgarity, " constantly besetting those who are half " conscious that they are in danger of it, " drives them into the opposite extreme of " affected finery."

Whately's style is as luminous as his writings are voluminous. His page is a beautiful mosaic ; and passages which a less artistic eye would have cast in foot-notes, are welded into the text. But, on the other hand, he sometimes marred effect by the use of parentheses, though no one more clearly saw this defect in the writings of others. " The censure of frequent and long paren- " theses," he said, " has led writers into the " preposterous expedient of leaving out the " marks by which they are indicated. It is " no cure to a lame man to take away his " crutches."

Dr. Whately had also an odd way of em- phasizing his words by the use of italics, but not to an extent to offend the eye ; and some might regard this womanly habit as a not in- harmonious alliance with his masculine sense.

As a logician, he reminded one of a porcupine bristling all over with points. In his chapter on Fallacies, he tells the reader always " to endeavour to put yourself in the " place of an opponent to your own argu- " ments, and consider whether you could not " find some objections to them."*

* " Elements of Logic," p. 175.

True to this principle, he was always on the defensive, engaged in parrying, with Spartan vigour, the strokes of a self-created adversary. In this way the myriads of Xerxes who sometimes pursued him, met more than their match.

With an Aristotelian disregard of the authority of antecedent speculation, he echoed the leading views of Paley and Warburton, and declared war to the knife against contemporary thinkers—Arnold and some few others perhaps excepted.

As a moralist, Dr. Whately practised what he preached; in laying down rules for preaching, he failed to practise what he preached. His sermons gave offence from their physiological and metaphysical drift. In his writings he reprobated " the practice, com-
" mon with many divines, of setting forth
" physiological or metaphysical theories as
" part of the Christian revelation, or as
" connected with it.*

---

* " Lectures and Reviews," p. 14. More than one person stupidly confounded this book with " Essays and " Reviews," and the Archbishop, as may be supposed, was justly savage at the mistake, which involved an imputation as well as a blunder.

Of his theological system, a Churchman tells us that it was essentially elenchical. In " this way we are favoured with disquisitions, " now on peculiarities, now on errors, now on " objections, now on dangers, and so forth. " Dr. Whately had a sort of mania for mental " dissection, and made every system pass " under the incisions of his argumentative " knife. The misfortune was that he could " cleave in sunder what he could not again " unite, leaving it mutilated and bleeding. " Now it may no doubt be the case with " many of the dogmatic school, that they " commence to build and are not able to " finish; but it is likewise true of Dr. " Whately that he began to pull down and " was not able to reconstruct. He brought " a vigorous and independent intellect to " bear on the phenomena of Revelation ; " and his mind, recoiling from traditional " opinions, struck at the current theology " till he laid it in ruins. But what did he " give us in its place ? Alas ! nothing but " negations, the drift of which were to prove, " not what Christianity was, but what it " was not."

Much of Dr. Whately's intense unpopularity

as a divine was owing to the rash eccentricity
with which in the social circle he loved to
drop exaggerated specimens of his theological
laxity. At a dinner party at Dr. B——'s,
his Grace mentioned that he had on that day
received a long letter from a " Religious In-
" quirer" in America, who requested that Dr.
Whately, as one of the highest theological
authorities, would recommend him a good
theological system. " My reply was laconic,"
remarked the Archbishop ; " I told him that
" I knew of no good system of theology."

Dr. Whately had a higher reputation in
America than nearer home. " American
" scholars," says the *Morning Post*, "give him
" equal rank with Butler, Watson, and Paley,
" one writer going so far as to say that he is
" the only Anglican bishop whose name will
" live."

But a recorded remark of his own reminds
us that we ought not to probe his idiosyncrasy
too minutely. " Some men are so excessively
" acute at detecting imperfections," he
writes, " that they scarcely notice *excel-*
" *lencies*. In looking at a peacock's train,
" they would fix on every spot where the

" feathers were worn, or the colours faded,
" and see nothing else."

To the Archbishop's " excellencies " we
must therefore look. One of his clergy,
addressing the writer of these pages,
says :—

" I give you briefly what I conceive to be
" the prominent excellencies in the character
" of my late Archbishop. First, inflexibility.
" He was careful to ascertain the right course
" of conduct ; he very seldom acted precipi-
" tantly ; he reflected long ; and consulted,
" I believe, the wisest authors ; but when
" his opinion was once settled—to adopt the
" remark which I remember having been
" made of him on a particular occasion—
" ' nothing could move him.' This rendered
" his conduct remarkably uniform and steady ;
" for, on all questions of importance, his
" opinion had been settled ; he appeared to be
" precisely the person described by the an-
" cient moralist :—

———" ' Fixed and steady to his trust ;
" ' Inflexible to truth, and obstinately just.'

" No one was ever more accommodating
" to the inclinations of others on occasions

" that did not involve moral principle. He
" united, in an eminent degree, steadfastness
" of purpose with gentleness of manner—
" the *suaviter in modo* and the *fortiter in*
" *re.*" *

If the old prelate wore the sting, he also bore
the honey. "As a prelate," writes another
of his clergy, "he was, though vigilant, mild,
" gentle, and paternal, ever leaning to the
" favourable interpretation; and as a ruler
" of men, he had that rare instinctive Nelson-
" gift of winning the heartiest work from all
" placed under his command."

Another cleric, the Rev. Dr. Salmon, observes:—" Only those more intimately ac-
" quainted with him knew how much there
" was in him to be loved. They have lost in
" him one of the truest and sincerest of
" friends, whose confidence, if not lightly
" bestowed, was not easily shaken, and who,
" indeed, was apt to form of the merits of
" those he loved what they themselves felt
" to be an over-indulgent estimate; and,
" perhaps, even they will own that they had

* Letter from Rev. James Burnett, dated Clonmethan
Glebe, co. Dublin, May 4th, 1864.

" not known all his claims on their affec-
" tionate regard until his tedious and painful
" illness revealed many a gentler grace, for
" the display of which there had been no
" opportunity before."

" It was a peculiarity in his nature, as it was
" in that of Swift," writes one who had nar-
rowly scanned this prelate, " that the interest
" with which he chose to cast his lot became
" a part of himself. To his mind, its rights
" became clear as those of his personal
" existence, and were to be fought for like
" his life. The metaphysician might have
" referred this characteristic to his pride, his
" courage, and especially to that unconscious
" egotism which towered above his other
" qualities, and, when he happened to be
" right, sometimes reached a pitch that was
" almost heroic."

APPENDIX.

The following is a List of the chief Writings of Dr. Whately.

Bacon's Essays, with Annotations. Five Editions.
Paley's Moral Philosophy, with Annotations.
Paley's Evidences of Christianity, with Annotations.
Elements of Logic. Nine Editions.
Elements of Rhetoric. Seven Editions.
Introductory Lectures on Political Economy, with Re-
    marks on Tithes, and on Poor-Laws, and on Penal
    Colonies. Four Editions.
Historic Doubts relative to Napoleon Buonaparte. Four-
    teen Editions.
Easy Lessons on Reasoning. Nine Editions.
Easy Lessons on Money Matters, for the Use of Young
    People. Fifteen Editions.
Introductory Lessons on Morals. Two Editions.
Introductory Lessons on the British Constitution. Two
    Editions.
Introductory Lessons on Mind.
Explanations of the Bible and of the Prayer Book.
The Scripture Doctrine concerning the Sacraments.
Lectures on the Characters of our Lord's Apostles. By
    a Country Pastor. Three Editions.
Lectures on the Scripture Revelations respecting Good
    and Evil Angels. Two Editions.
View of the Scripture Revelations respecting a Future
    State. Eight Editions.

Lectures on Prayer.

The Parish Pastor.

The Kingdom of Christ delineated, in Two Essays on our Lord's own Account of his Person, and of the Nature of his Kingdom, and on the Constitution, Powers, and Ministry of a Christian Church, as appointed by Himself. Six Editions.

Essays (First Series) on some of the Peculiarities of the Christian Religion. Seven Editions.

Essays (Second Series) on some of the Difficulties in the Writings of the Apostle Paul, and in other parts of the New Testament. Eight Editions.

Essays (Third Series) on the Errors of Romanism having their Origin in Human Nature. Five Editions.

Essays on some of the Dangers to Christian Faith which may arise from the Teaching or the Conduct of its Professors. Three Editions.

The Use and Abuse of Party-Feeling in Matters of Religion, considered in Eight Sermons preached in the year 1822, at the Bampton Lecture. To which are added Five Sermons preached before the University of Oxford. And a Discourse by Archbishop King, with Notes and Appendix. Four Editions.

Charges and other Tracts. 8vo.

Sermons on various Subjects. Three Editions.

Thoughts on the Sabbath; to which is subjoined, An Address to the Inhabitants of Dublin, on the Observance of the Lord's Day. Four Editions.

Address to the Clergy and other Members of the Established Church, on the Use and Abuse of the Present Occasion for the Exercise of Beneficence. Two Editions.

Expected Restoration of the Jews, and the Millennium.

Being the Seventh Lecture of *A View of the Scripture Revelations concerning a Future State.*

Preparation for Death. Being the Twelfth Lecture of *A View of the Scripture Revelations concerning a Future State.*

Introductory Lessons on Christian Evidences.* Fourteen Editions.

The same Work in French, Italian, Spanish, German, Swedish, Greek, and Hebrew.

Introductory Lessons on the History of Religious Worship,† being a Sequel to the Lessons on Christian Evidences. Two Editions.

The same Work in French and Italian.

Thoughts on Secondary Punishment, in a Letter to Earl Grey. pp. 204.

Remarks on Transportation. pp. 172.

Sermons on Various Subjects, delivered in several Churches in Dublin. pp. 572.

The Light and the Life; or the History of Him whose Name we Bear.

Christian Evidences.

Scripture Doctrine concerning the Sacraments.

Lectures on Prayer. By a Country Pastor. pp. 194.

The Parish Pastor. pp. 326—pub. 1860.

Some Reminiscences of the Life of the late Edward Copleston, Bishop of Llandaff. 1854.

Sacra Domestica; a Course of Family Prayers.

Lectures on Scripture Parables. By Mrs. Whately, with the Correction and Supervision of Dr. Whately.

---

* Questions deducible from the Introductory Lessons on Christian Evidences. By Henry Edward Jolly, D.D.

† Questions deducible from the Introductory Lessons on the History of Religious Worship.

A Short Account of the First Preaching of the Gospel
by the Apostles, being a Continuation of " Conversa-
tions on the Life of Jesus Christ." By a Mother.
Pub. 1830.

Miscellaneous Lectures and Reviews.

Cautions for the Times. Edited by the Archbishop of
Dublin.

Outlines of Mythology. By a Scholar of Trinity College, Dublin. With an Account of the Character and
Origin of the Pagan Religions, extracted by permission
from the Writings of the Archbishop of Dublin.

English Synonyms. Edited by R. Whately, D.D., Archbishop of Dublin. Four Editions.

Chance and Choice ; or, the Education of Circumstances.
Two Tales : 1. The Young Governess.— 2. Claudine
de Soligny.

Expedition to New Holland [partly written by Dr.
Whately], with a considerable number of Charges,
addressed to the Clergy of the Dioceses of Dublin,
Glendalough, and Kildare.

Six Dramas, illustrative of German Life, from the original
of the Princess Amalie of Saxony. With Frontis-
pieces. Post 8vo. [Attributed to Dr. Whately.]

English Life, Social and Domestic, in the middle of the
Nineteenth Century. [Attributed to Dr. Whately.]

Remarks on some of the Characters of Shakespeare, by
T. Whately, Esq. Edited by R. Whately, D.D., Archbishop of Dublin.

Reverses ; or, Memoirs of the Fairfax Family. By the
Author of *English Life.* [Attributed to Dr. Whately.]

Second Part of the History of Rasselas, Prince of Abys-
sinia. [Attributed to Dr. Whately.]

Proverbs and Precepts, for Copy Lines.

DR. HAWKINS.

(Vol. I. p. 8.)

With Hawkins, Whately was generally associated hand in hand. Both were noted at Oxford for upholding the doctrine of tradition. Dr. Hawkins, in a celebrated sermon on that subject, lays down a proposition that the sacred Scripture was never intended to teach doctrine, but only to prove it, and that one must resort to the formularies of the Church, including the Catechism and Creeds, in order to learn doctrine. In this view Dr. Whately then warmly concurred. It struck at the root of the Bible Society, which possessed a strong auxiliary association at Oxford, and to which most of the leading fellows, including Newman, had lent their names and purse. Whately afterwards rather wandered from his original views on tradition. "Many," he said, in his own amusing and unthcological way, " defend oral tradition on the " ground that we have the Scriptures themselves by tradi- " tion. Would they think that because they might trust " servants to deliver a letter, however long or important, " therefore they might trust them to deliver its contents " by word of mouth in a message ? A footman brings " you a letter from a friend, upon whose word you can " perfectly rely, giving an account of something that has " happened to himself, and the exact account of which " you are greatly concerned to know. While you are " reading and answering the letter, the footman goes into " the kitchen, and there gives your cook an account of " the same thing ; which, he says, he overheard the " upper servants at home talking over, as related to them " by the valet, who said he had it from your friend's " son's own lips."

www.ingramcontent.com/pod-product-compliance
Lightning Source LLC
Chambersburg PA
CBHW020322140726
47905CB00013B/2145